"Hi, honey, I'm home!"

Aiden heard her laugh and followed it to the nursery, where she stood on a ladder. "Be careful." He extended a hand to help her down. Good thing, because she faltered and fell into him. "See, this is why you need me," he said, catching her.

He pulled her closer and lowered his head toward her, hesitating, giving her a chance to object.

Their first kiss had been for the tabloid reporter. This kiss wasn't for show. This one had been a long time coming.

Need coursed through him, unlike any he'd ever felt. Never in his long history of women, each of whom was supposed to be the antidote for Bia. But there was no antidote.

There had always been obstacles between them—physical distance, engagements, his marriage and their jobs. Till now.

Enough was enough. This time he was claiming what was his.

* * *

Celebrations, Inc: Let's get this party started!

W9-AMT-373

Dear Reader,

Are you familiar with the Voltaire proverb "Perfect is the enemy of very good"? He contended that waiting for perfection causes you to miss out on the good things in life.

That's almost the case with the heroine of *Celebration's Baby*. Bia Anderson is so preoccupied with perfection (read: not getting hurt) that she nearly misses out on the wonderful man who has been right under her nose most of her life. Thank goodness Aiden Woods recognizes a good thing when he sees it. He is the ideal blend of patient and persistence. Pretty soon, Bia realizes that the man for her has been with her all along.

There's an added bonus in this book. Maya (the chocolate maker) figures prominently. I don't want to spoil anything, but there are some pretty nice surprises in store for her, too.

I hope you'll love Bia and Aiden's (and Maya's) story as much as I enjoyed writing it. I always love hearing from readers. You can connect with me through my website, www.nancyrobardsthompson.com; Twitter, @NRTWrites; and Facebook, www.facebook.com/NRobardsThompson.

Warmly,

Nancy

Celebration's Baby

—

Nancy Robards Thompson

H HARLEQUIN® SPECIAL EDITION®

Recycling programs
for this product may
not exist in your area.

ISBN-13: 978-0-373-65809-1

CELEBRATION'S BABY

Copyright © 2014 by Nancy Robards Thompson

Printed in U.S.A.

NANCY ROBARDS THOMPSON

Award-winning author Nancy Robards Thompson is a sister, wife and mother who has lived the majority of her life south of the Mason-Dixon line. As the oldest sibling, she reveled in her ability to make her brother laugh at inappropriate moments, and she soon learned she could get away with it by proclaiming, "What? I wasn't doing anything." It's no wonder that upon graduating from college with a degree in journalism, she discovered that reporting "just the facts" bored her silly. Since she hung up her press pass to write novels full-time, critics have deemed her books "funny, smart and observant." She loves chocolate, champagne, cats and art (though not necessarily in that order). When she's not writing, she enjoys spending time with her family, reading, hiking and doing yoga.

This book is dedicated with love to good friends
who are steadfast and true.

Chapter One

Being in charge had its perks. Today, Bia Anderson fully intended to cash in. After all, there was chocolate involved.

She lifted her chin a little higher as she walked up the petunia-lined path to the old bungalow located at the end of Main Street in downtown Celebration—the new home of Maya's Chocolates.

Nicole Harrison, a staff writer for the *Dallas Journal of Business and Development,* where Bia was the editor in chief, hadn't hidden her disappointment that morning. Bia had assigned her to the catch-a-greased-pig contest at the grand opening of the Piggly Wiggly over in Kenansville rather than the interview for the Maya's Chocolates business profile.

It wasn't the first time she and Nicole had butted

heads, and it probably wouldn't be the last. But that came with the territory. In the two months since Bia had taken the reins as editor of the paper, making tough calls that sometimes disappointed the staff hadn't gotten easier, but she just had to suck it up and do what she thought was best.

So what if they all thought she was hard as nails, lacking empathy and compassion?

What would they think when they found out she was going to be a mother? The wall immediately went up, and she told herself she didn't care what they'd say or do or how they'd smirk when they learned she was pregnant by *People*'s reigning "Sexiest Man Alive," Hugh Newman. The thought knocked the air out of her. And not in a good way; it was more like a sucker punch to the gut. Reflexively, her hand went to her belly.

She'd done the pregnancy test last night, finally pulling her head out of the sand after being two months late. She still hadn't quite wrapped her mind around the reality of it—although the unexpected pregnancy did explain why she'd been craving chocolate to the point of insanity.

At first, she'd blamed the cravings on the stress of the Hugh Newman debacle: a five-day lapse of judgment that had ended abruptly when the paparazzi started inquiring into the identity of the woman with the auburn hair in the blue sundress, with whom Newman had been seen *canoodling* in Celebration, Texas.

Canoodling? Did anyone even use that word anymore?

He'd been in town doing location research—

soaking up local color for his next movie. Also, he had accepted an invitation to emcee the annual Doctor's Charity Ball, which benefited the new pediatric surgical wing at Celebration Memorial Hospital. Bia had gotten an up-close-and-personal tutorial of why Hugh had been named Mr. Sexy when she'd had lunch with him to interview him for the paper (and you can bet Nicole Harrison hadn't been happy that Bia had claimed that assignment). Five minutes into the interview, Hugh Newman had charmed the pants off her. Okay, so maybe it had been more like an hour. God, she wasn't *that* easy.

Bia stepped onto the porch and tried the door. It was locked. So she knocked and waited for Maya to let her in.

Truth be told, Bia wasn't easy at all.

At twenty-eight years old, she'd only had two lovers. Her first had been Duane, as part of a six-year relationship that had ended in a broken engagement; the other was Hugh, an impetuous mistake she'd known wouldn't last. And, of course, it hadn't.

She just hadn't expected to walk away with such a personal memento of their time together.

Dammit, she'd simply wanted one taste of sexy. *One taste*—and she had been prepared to walk away. But one night became five and then the media had gotten wind of the affair and suddenly the entire world was dying to know the identity of the woman with the auburn hair in the blue sundress. Overnight, Bia had gone from relative obscurity to the top of *XYZ Celebrity News*'s most-stalked list.

She did a hasty scan of the area looking for skulking media-types. It was a beautiful day. Shoppers were wandering in and out of places like On a Roll Bakery, Three Sisters dress shop, Dolce Vita Gourmet Grocery and Barbara's Beauty Salon. But the area was all clear of lurking *XYZ* minions. Oh, they were gone now, thank God. The paparazzi had lost interest when Hugh's camp had explained that the redhead in the blue sundress was simply his tour guide.

Nothing to see here, folks. Just a tour guide.

Liar, liar, sexy pants on fire.

At least they hadn't called her an escort.

What had really burned was when Hugh's people had offered to pay her to keep her mouth shut. She didn't want his money. But she did want her privacy back. That's the only reason she'd agreed to play along with the tour guide charade. Still, she told them to pass along the message that Hugh could keep his money and the insult it implied.

Within hours of explaining Bia away, Hugh and his longtime on-again, off-again starlet girlfriend, Kristin Capistrano, announced that they were, indeed, on again. *How lovely for them.* Then the tabloids developed instant amnesia about the "tour guide" and were all ablaze with the news that they had a "liftoff" and that "Hugh-stin" certainly did not have a problem. The pair proclaimed they were deeply in love and— surprise surprise—that Kristin would be costarring with Hugh in the movie that was filming in Celebration, Texas. The one for which he'd been soaking up the local color when he'd met Bia.

Bia's mouth went dry as she thought of the scandal it would cause if anyone found out the sexiest man alive was her baby daddy.

She clenched her fists, digging her nails into her palms. As far as she was concerned, Hugh Newman was dead to her. But the blue line on the pregnancy test had resurrected him.

Now she wasn't sure what to do… Except that, ready or not, she was going to have a baby—and she was going to keep it.

There was no question about that. Bia was adopted, and she'd often wondered why her birth mother had chosen to give her up rather than trying to make it work. Her mother and father—the ones who had adopted her—had been good people. At least her father had been. She hadn't really known her adoptive mother. She'd passed away when Bia was five, leaving her adoptive father to raise her.

The strong, silent type, he'd never been much of a talker. He'd bristled the handful of times she'd asked about her birth mother. So she hadn't pressed it.

Her dad had passed away last year, and now more than ever she wished she knew more about her roots. Maybe it was time to start digging. She'd need to know…for her child's sake. Health history and all that.

Bia rapped on the door again, shifting her weight from one foot to another. Across the street, a friend of her father's called to her and waved. She waved back.

Thank God her father wasn't alive to see what a mess she'd made of things. She sighed.

It had just *happened*. When she'd sat down to interview Hugh, she'd been the picture of professionalism. At first she'd been immune to his notorious charms.

Then he'd started putting the moves on her. Heavy-duty flirting. With her.

Hugh Newman had been flirting with *her*.

That was all it had taken for her resolve to melt like pure cane sugar in hot-brewed tea.

They'd used protection. Every single time.

That's the part she couldn't quite comprehend. How this could have happened when she'd been so careful?

Thinking about it made her feel nauseated.

She gave herself a mental shake.

She'd made her choices. Now she'd have to live with the consequences. Still, if she could just have one do-over in life, she'd turn back the clock two months and stay the heck away from Mr. Sexy. She'd let Nicole be Hugh Newman's *tour guide*.

She knocked on the door yet again, this time a little harder. Where the heck was Maya?

Above Bia's head hung a weathered, hand-painted wooden sign that boasted, Maya's Chocolates—Happily Ever After Starts Here. It swayed and squeaked on the lazy breeze of the warm May afternoon. The words, written in gray-blue calligraphy on a whitewashed background, were underlined by a fancy, scrolling arrow that pointed toward the door.

Happily Ever After. Right here, huh?

Nice thought.

She tried the door again, this time giving it a firmer tug and then a push, but it was locked tight as a tick. She shaded her eyes and peered in the glass front door. No one was in the showroom. All the fixtures seemed to be in place, but they looked empty.

Hmm, that was curious.

The store's grand opening was scheduled for next week. Bia thought that a good bit of the merchandise would be in place by now.

Had Maya forgotten their appointment? If they didn't let her in to start the interview soon, Bia couldn't promise that anyone was going to have a happily ever after. Bia glanced at her cell phone to check the time. Okay, so she was a couple of minutes early, but it was warm outside. She was feeling a little dizzy and beads of perspiration were forming underneath her silk blouse and starting to run down the crevice of her back.

Certain foods and smells—like coffee and the noxious traffic fumes wafting up from Main Street—made her feel ill. That, along with the chocolate cravings and, of course, the missed periods, were what had finally sent her to Dallas to purchase the in-home test. She couldn't purchase it in the local drugstore. Word would get around faster than if it had been aired on *XYZ*.

She blinked away the thought and refocused on the mental list of interview questions she would ask Maya…if she ever answered the door.

Bia was just about to dial Maya's phone number when, through the panes of glass on the front door, she saw the woman hurrying toward her in a flurry of long red spiral curls and flouncing green scarf and skirt. She was wiping her hands on a dish towel, which she flung over her shoulder as she opened the door with a breathless greeting.

"*Bonjour!* You're here!" Maya's lyrical accented voice rang out and mingled with the sounds of chirping birds and traffic. "I hope you have not been waiting long. I was in the kitchen putting the finishing touches on a surprise just for you. Come in! Come in, *cher!* Please, come in."

A surprise? For me?

"I hope it's chocolate," Bia said.

"But of course it is." Maya smiled as she held open the door for Bia and motioned her inside. A cool gust of air that smelled like rich dark chocolate greeted her and took the edge off her queasiness. Bia breathed in deeply.

"Well, then, in that case, you're forgiven." Bia grinned. "I have been dreaming of your chocolate since the Doctor's Ball. It was the first time I'd tasted it. In fact, for the past several weeks, I've been craving chocolate like crazy, but the over-the-counter stuff just isn't doing it for me. I think you've spoiled me for all other sweets. I just learned that Baldoon's Pub offers your Irish cream truffles on their dessert menu."

"Indeed they do," Maya said over her shoulder as Bia followed her into the house. "I like to hear that I've spoiled you for other chocolate. You might say that's the theme of my business plan."

The front room was set up as a shop with a refrigerated glass case in the center of the space. Like the shelving fixtures, the case was empty, Bia noted with chagrin. But it was surrounded by lovely silver-veined marble counters that housed a cash register and supplies to wrap purchases. Even if there was a decided dearth of chocolate, the place looked fresh and clean and light with its white paint, whitewashed wooden floors and yards of silver tulle draped elegantly across the ceiling. The look created an ethereal cloudlike effect.

Again, Bia breathed in the delicious aroma of chocolate, and her stomach growled. Since the cases and shelves were empty, she had to wonder if she was imagining the scent. Or had Maya piped it in for effect?

"Where's the chocolate?" Bia finally asked. "Don't you make all your goods on the premises? If so, how are you going to fill the cases and shelves before the grand opening?"

Maya glanced around the room. "I suppose it does look rather empty in here, doesn't it?" She sighed and went behind the wrap stand. "Alas, the increased demand for chocolate has forced me to be less hands-on with the manufacturing process. I still make some special made-to-order candy—like this batch I made especially for you this morning."

She presented a three-tiered glass-and-silver dessert plate brimming with confections in various shapes and colors. Bia's mouth watered at the sight.

"I thought I smelled chocolate in the air. But then I worried that I'd simply imagined it."

Maya laughed. "It is a lovely fragrance, isn't it? Some say the mere smell of chocolate causes a woman's body to release hormones that simulate the feeling of falling in love."

"Ha! All of the feelings and none of the heartache," Bia said. "Sounds like the perfect relationship. I just wish chocolate didn't love me back so much. It tends to stay with me. You know, right here." She patted her left hip.

"I don't know what you're talking about, you are reed-thin. You have nothing to worry about."

"Gosh, makes chocolates, gives compliments…I think you and I could be good friends."

Maya's eyes shone. "I certainly hope so."

"You will have chocolate for the grand opening, won't you?" Bia asked.

Maya nodded. "Of course. I was fortunate enough to find a stateside manufacturer who was able to duplicate my family recipe in bulk, the one my grandmother used to start the business three generations ago. The candy for the shelves and case will be delivered the day before we open. That way it will be as fresh as can be. We'll have to work extra hard to get everything in place, but it will be worth it."

Maya gestured toward the plate. "But please, don't let me detain you. Help yourself."

Reverently, Bia approached the manna. She paused to give the illusion of self-control, so that it didn't look as if she was about to bury her face in all that deliciousness. But then she found herself genuinely appreciating the sheer artistry of Maya's offering.

Yes, this definitely could be the start of a beautiful friendship.

Maya placed a silver cocktail napkin on the counter next to Bia. She also produced a small crystal pitcher of water, a matching glass and a plate containing bread, crackers and apple slices.

"What is this?" Bia asked.

"These are the palate cleansers for the chocolate tasting," Maya said. "To fully discern the differences between the chocolates, you must cleanse your palate between each tasting."

Oh. Bia suddenly felt a little out of her element. "You treat chocolate like some people treat wine?"

"Pourquoi pas?" Maya asked.

"You're right. Why not?"

"May I recommend that you start with the chocolates on the first tier? It has a lower percentage of cocoa and a milder taste. The chocolate on the upper tier will overpower those on the bottom. I suggest you let the chocolate melt on your tongue rather than chewing it, and in between different bites, enjoy a bit of apple or bread washed down by the water. That way you will taste all the nuances of each piece."

Maya gestured to the plate and gave Bia a few more tips on how to proceed: to observe the chocolate, to smell it and to break it, feeling the way the pieces of solid chocolate snapped, before finally tasting it. Those were all indicators of good quality.

Finally, she said, "That is enough instruction. Please enjoy."

Bia started to choose a chocolate from the bottom, but she paused. "Will there be a quiz when I'm finished?"

Maya laughed her perfect, crystal laugh. Bia breathed in deeply, savoring the mélange of scents from the plate. For the first time in a long time, a sense of peace and well-being washed over her.

"Only questions about which are your favorites," Maya answered.

"It's all gorgeous. I'm sure they will all be delicious."

First, she selected what looked like a classic chocolate truffle dusted with cocoa powder. She bit into it, and flavor exploded on her tongue. She closed her eyes and had to make a conscious effort not to let a moan escape.

Oh, Maya was wrong. This chocolate didn't simulate love; it was better. Way better. Better than kissing. Better than sex.

Oh, my God, I'm in public and I'm making virtual love to a French truffle. And I don't care.

She opened her eyes, and her gaze automatically found the dessert plate. She was tempted to pluck up another piece—a handful—even before she had finished the first. Somehow she managed to restrain herself.

She popped the rest of the first truffle into her mouth. She had the same urge to moan over the chocolate. It was too good. So she quit fighting and gave in to the unadulterated pleasure.

Finally, after blissfully indulging in several pieces from each level, Bia forced herself to take a step back. She had to put some space between herself and her vice. If she didn't, she was going to eat too much. Although, with the lingering flavors of chocolate, orange, cinnamon and cloves teasing her taste buds, that seemed unlikely. With one last wistful glance at the candy, she said, "That was delicious, Maya. I wish I could say I'd eaten myself sick, but I think I may want more later."

"And you say that like it's a bad thing?"

The two laughed like old friends.

"Your decor looks exquisite. Who did your decorating?"

Maya beamed. "Thank you. I did it myself. I tried to give the front of the house a similar feel to my shop in St. Michel. Similar, but maybe a touch more modern. More American. I wanted it to feel like home, since I will be spending a great deal of time here."

"Let's see," Bia said, flipping through her reporter's notebook, searching for the brief bio she'd gathered on Maya. "You're from St. Michel in Europe. Are you moving to Celebration?"

Maya stopped, considering the question. "I will be here for the time being. Because my heart is telling me Celebration is where I belong right now, especially while I am getting the new location off the ground. I must make sure it does well."

Bia jotted down more notes and anecdotes for use in her story. "Who is looking after your St. Michel shop while you're away?"

"I have promoted my assistant, Grace, to the managerial position. If anyone knows the shop as well as I do, Grace does. I trust that the place is in good hands."

Maya paused again, as if weighing her words. "As you can imagine, the Celebration location will need much tender loving care while I get the business off the ground."

Bia nodded. "I'm curious, though. Why in the world did you choose Celebration, Texas, as the location of your first U.S. retail store? I mean, no offense to this town. It's a great place. It's my home. But of all the places in the world…why Celebration?"

Maya's eyes shone as she regarded Bia, and for

the first time Bia noticed that the older woman's eyes were a gorgeous shade of hazel infused with intriguing flecks of amber and green, accentuated by the color of her skirt. The same mossy color was also echoed in the silk scarf that she had artfully arranged around her neck. *Leave it to the French,* Bia mused. They could create something enchanted out of a yard of silk and a bolt of tulle.

Maya's hair was magical, too. Bia's hair, when left to its natural devices, was almost as curly as Maya's. But Bia straightened hers since it never wanted to do the same thing twice. A few months ago, she'd opted for a keratin treatment so she wouldn't have to fight with it during the humid days of summer. It was only May, but the oppressive damp-heat days were already bearing down on them, as if someone were misting the entire town with a gigantic vaporizer. At this rate, by the time August rolled around, humidity would hang in the air like a billowing stratus cloud. Thanks to the magic of keratin, at least Bia's hair was armed and ready to take on the summer…and the pregnancy.

Oh…the pregnancy.

She swallowed hard and blinked away the thought.

"Why Celebration?" Bia urged.

She looked up from her notepad and caught Maya staring at her with an odd expression. In an instant the look was gone, replaced by Maya's placid, Madonna-like smile.

"I have…friends here. Do you know Pepper Meriweather, A. J. Sherwood-Antonelli and Caroline Coopersmith?" Maya asked.

"I know Caroline. Her husband, Drew Montgomery, is my boss."

Maya gave a quick flick of her wrist. "Of course he is. Well, I met Caroline, A.J. and Pepper through a mutual friend who went to school with them. This was a few years ago, before any of them were married. They'd come to St. Michel to help another friend. Margeaux Broussard? Do you know her?"

Bia shook her head and continued to furiously scribble notes as Maya talked.

"Anyhow," Maya continued, "the girls had come to St. Michel with Margeaux to help her make amends with her father, from whom she'd been estranged for the better part of her life. Once they'd accomplished that mission, they returned to Celebration, luring my good friend Sydney James away from St. Michel with the promise of a job with Texas Star Energy right here in Celebration."

Bia raised her head and looked at Maya. She knew Sydney pretty well, since the woman had just married Miles Mercer. Miles was good friends with Bia's best friend, Aiden Woods. The four of them got together a lot. Bia would've called it double dating if she and Aiden had been a couple, but they weren't. She'd known him since kindergarten and cared too much about him to ruin their relationship by dating him.

"Texas Star Energy, huh?" Bia said.

Maya nodded and quirked a brow that seemed to indicate she knew all about the scandalous demise of the corrupt energy empire. Bia had been the reporter who had broken the story that had started the conglomerate's unraveling. In fact, her investigative reporting and subsequent awards had helped her clinch the editorship of the paper after Drew Montgomery had decided to give up editing to focus more on the publishing end of the paper. But Texas Star was in the past. It was a can of worms Bia didn't want to reopen.

"So, you followed your friends to Celebration?"

"Oh, *mais non.* It's a little more complicated." Maya pursed her lips. "At first, I visited them. I attended each of their weddings. In fact, some might say that I even had a hand in bringing each of them together with their soul mates."

"You introduced them?"

Maya gave a noncommittal one-shoulder shrug. How very French her gestures were. But wait…hadn't Drew met Caroline at a wedding…? Yes. It had been Caroline's sister's wedding. It had been right around the time that everything was coming to a head at Texas Star.

"Technically, *non.* I didn't physically introduce them. It's another complicated story, really."

"You're full of complicated stories, aren't you? If you'd care to expound, I'm here to listen…. That's what I do."

Maya studied her as if she was deciding whether she would take Bia up on the offer of a listening ear.

"Well, I do love to talk." Maya laughed, an infectious sound that made Bia smile.

"Over the years, the girls—Pepper, A.J. and Caroline—have become very dear to me. So, I've always looked out for them, and that's how I had a hand in bringing them together with their soul mates."

Again, Bia paused and looked up at the woman.

Soul mates. There was that word again. Bia filed soul mates in the same category as happily ever after. She wasn't sure she believed there was such a thing, especially after being left at the altar by the man who should've been her *soul mate* if there was such a thing. Nope, in her book, love was an urban legend. People talked about it. Some even claimed to have experienced it, but *real* love—the kind that grafted your soul to another person's for better or worse, the type that could withstand bleached-blonde strippers and the relentless paparazzi—had managed to elude Bia her entire life.

Actually, she'd read somewhere that soul mates weren't always lovers. Sometimes they were parent and child, sometimes best friends. If that were true, the closest thing to a soul mate she'd ever had was Aiden. Their relationship had survived some pretty treacherous hurdles. It had actually transcended sex. That's probably why it worked. They hadn't ruined things by getting physical.

God knew there had been plenty of times Bia had been tempted to give in to his charm. The guy was gorgeous—in a more rugged and down-to-earth way than Hugh's pretty-boy looks. Women found Aiden irresistible. Since college, he'd had a constant rotation of babes. None of them serious.

Then he'd gotten married. It had lasted two years before they'd called it quits and he'd reverted back to his freewheeling ways.

He wouldn't talk about what had happened. All he would say was that he hadn't cheated. "It just didn't work out."

His smorgasbord of women had been the main reason Bia had kept Aiden in the friend zone. Well, that and the fact that he'd thrown the bachelor party that ended with the stripper that had broken up her engagement.

Still, despite all Aiden's faults, Duane and Hugh were long gone, and Aiden was still there.

She put her hand on her stomach. And he would be the first person she told about the baby.

"…and I came to Celebration to see each one of them say I do," Maya continued. "Each time I visited, I was drawn to this town. As time went on and I visited more, I knew there was a reason I was supposed to be here."

For a moment, Maya looked wistful. Bia studied her, taking a mental snapshot and hoping she could somehow convey Maya's mood in the article.

"Would you care to elaborate?"

A warm smile reclaimed Maya's delicate features. "At home, in St. Michel, I'm known as *un marieur*."

"I beg your pardon," said Bia.

"A matchmaker. I am a third-generation chocolatier by trade, but matchmaking, you might say, is my passion. Some people believe my chocolate is magical."

Bia stopped writing and looked up. The cinnamon and clove from the last piece of chocolate still lingered on the back of her tongue.

"So, you're telling me your chocolate is enchanted? What? Do you sprinkle in love potions or something?"

"I would claim nothing of the sort. My chocolate is all natural. Everything is on the label, except for a few proprietary blends."

"The love potions?"

Maya raked her hands through her hair. "Oh, I should not have said that. Please don't print that in the profile."

"Why not? It will probably drive business through the roof. Everyone wants love."

Well, almost everyone.

As if confirming Bia's thoughts, Maya did her one-shoulder French shrug.

"What?" Bia asked. "You don't believe that?"

"I do believe there is someone for everyone. You, for instance. You've had your share of setbacks, but there's someone for you. In fact, you've already met him."

Whoa. Whoa. Whoa. If she was going to start asking about the Hugh Newman debacle, Bia would shut that down very quickly. Instead of waiting to get caught in the pickle, she turned the tables.

"Is there someone special in *your* life?"

Maya paused and drew in a slow, thoughtful breath.

Ha. It's not so comfortable to be on the receiving end of the dating game rapid-fire, is it?

"Alas, even though my intuition is generally good when it comes to pairing up others, it doesn't work so well for me personally."

"So, does this *intuitive gift* of yours carry over into other areas? Would you go as far as saying you have the gift of second sight?"

Maya laughed. "If I had the second sight, I would've already won the lottery. I wouldn't be agonizing over rollout budgets and marketing campaigns. But that's strictly off the record, *oui?*"

"Fair enough," said Bia. "Back to the business of chocolate. I understand this is the first of two new Maya's Chocolates that you're opening stateside. Where will the other location be?"

"I want to get the one here in Celebration off the ground, and then I'll look into opening another, possibly in New York. However, it's important that I ensure the fiscal health of the current locations. Especially the one in St. Michel. That's where my grandmother started the business. It has been a fixture in downtown St. Michel for three generations. All of the recipes have been passed down through the years from mother to daughter."

"And will you continue the tradition?"

Maya nodded.

"Do you have children?"

For a fraction of a second, Bia thought she saw a shade of sadness color Maya's eyes.

"Come with me," Maya said. "I want to show you something."

The woman led the way to the kitchen, which was hidden behind a double-layered curtain made of silver gossamer backed by heavy white satin. When Maya parted the drapes, allowing Bia her first glimpse behind the scenes, Bia half expected she would glimpse the great and powerful Oz or some other secret to which mere mortals weren't privy. If they were, wouldn't every chocoholic have her own in-home chocolatier?

But when Bia stepped over the threshold, she didn't see anything that looked extraordinary. In fact, the kitchen, with its sterile stainless-steel countertops and run-of-the-mill industrial sink, refrigerator and gas range, looked quite...ordinary. Well, with the exception of the gleaming copper pots hanging on a rack over the sink, and the adorable pink-and-black box that was festively tied with a ribbon and waiting on the counter. Bia eyed the package.

It looked like a box of Maya's famous chocolate.

For her to take home? She had to bite her tongue to keep from asking the question out loud.

As if Maya had read her mind, she picked up the package and handed it to Bia. "This is for you."

"Ah, thank you," Bia said.

She gestured around the kitchen with a motion of her hand. "So this is where the magic happens?"

Pride straightened Maya's already admirable posture. "*Oui.* My mother and grandmother passed on those copper pots over there. That's what I wanted to show you. The recipes are proprietary, guarded jealously and handed down through the generations with the copper pots and the family Bible, from mother to daughter to granddaughter."

She walked over and took down one of the three gleaming vessels, running the pads of her manicured fingers lovingly over its shiny surface. "My grandmother gave them to my mother, and, in turn, my mother gave them to me. Everything in this shop is brand-new, but I brought these with me as a symbol of the past, to remind me of the importance of family. I use them to make special smaller batches. Personal chocolates. Like those you sampled earlier and the box you will take home."

"Thank you," Bia said.

But the burning question, the one that Maya had quite deftly skirted, was the one about children. While Bia hated to assume, she couldn't bring herself to press Maya for an answer. Wasn't it obvious? If Maya had an heir, she would've said so. Judging by the look on her face when Bia had originally asked the question, she knew she'd struck a nerve. No, it was definitely better not to go there.

"Your grandmother founded the business? She named it Maya's Chocolates?"

"She did."

"So, you were named after the family business?"

"No, I was named after my grandmother. Her name was also Maya."

A bittersweet taste caught in the back of Bia's throat, replacing the cinnamon and cloves. How lucky Maya was to be so connected to her past. It was a luxury that might not be afforded to Bia, unless she chose to go out searching for the woman who'd given her up all those years ago. Would it really be worth it? Walking into someone's life, disrupting—or possibly upending—the world to which they'd become accustomed?

If an attempted reconnection ended in rejection, maybe it would be better to leave well enough alone. She'd had a happy childhood with a father who'd done his darnedest to give her the best life he was capable of giving. Maybe there was something wrong with wanting any more than that.

She put her hand on her stomach. If Bia could get blind health records from the adoption agency, maybe it would serve everyone best to look forward rather than backward.

"Do you have extended family who will carry on the Maya's Chocolates tradition in the future?"

"That remains to be seen."

There was that look again. Bia glimpsed it before Maya turned away to hang up the copper pot.

She was just about to ask Maya to clarify the *remains to be seen* comment, when a patch of cold sweat erupted on the back of Bia's neck. She tugged at the neckline of her dress. Good grief, it felt as if someone had turned up the heat in the kitchen at least twenty degrees. A dizzying wave of nausea passed over her, and she grabbed on to the edge of the counter to steady herself.

Maya reached out and touched Bia's arm. "Are you all right? Let me get you some water and a chair so you can sit down."

Maya pulled over a wrought-iron chair from a small glass-topped table for two that stood in the corner of the kitchen. Bia had been so busy ogling the box of chocolates she hadn't noticed the dining set until now. Shaking, she lowered herself onto the seat. What the heck was wrong with her? She'd heard of morning sickness, but it was midafternoon. This was ridiculous. She'd just have to power through. She had so much to do she didn't have time for the indulgence of a sick day. As she'd done since she'd first felt the symptoms, she made the choice to buck up and push through.

Mind over matter. She always managed to feel better when she decided not to think about how she felt, not to give in.

Maya returned with some ice water. Bia gratefully accepted it and took a sip. She pressed the cool glass to her forehead. It helped.

How embarrassing was this? She took a deep breath and reminded herself she just needed to tie up loose ends for the article and then she could leave. She might even work from home for the rest of the day as she wrote the story.

"Thank you, Maya. I'm sorry about the interruption. I'm just feeling a little light-headed."

Maya walked over and put a cool hand on Bia's cheek. The breach of personal space was a little startling, but at the same time, it was sort of touching.

"No fever," Maya said. "Here, give me your hand."

Bia hesitated for a moment, then complied. Maya held Bia's hand. If the hand on the cheek had been a little weird, this made Bia want to squirm. But the thought of moving caused a new wave of nausea to crest.

"Any chance you could be pregnant?" Maya asked with the same casual tone she might use if she were asking if Bia had ever tasted chocolate-dipped bacon.

Bia jerked her hand away from Maya's and tried to stand up, but the rush of blood to her head landed her right back on the chair—hard.

"That's a very personal question," Bia insisted as alarms sounded in her head: Maya and her intuition. But what audacity for the woman to even suggest something like that to someone she barely knew?

Bia stood, this time more carefully. "I need to go."

"I didn't mean to upset you," Maya said. "Please

know everything is going to be okay. You have to believe that—"

"I'm just under the weather," Bia said, a little too irritably. "It's nothing to be alarmed about."

Bia turned to leave but dropped her notebook as she tried to hitch her purse up on her shoulder.

Maya swooped down and retrieved the notebook before Bia could reach it. "Bia, I'm sorry." Maya handed it to her. Bia took it with a quick jerk of the hand. "Really. I didn't mean to upset you."

"Don't worry about it. I'll have Nicole Harrison call you if we need anything else for the article."

Maya nodded solemnly. "Please forgive me if I have overstepped my bounds. But I have to say this. Please know you and the baby are going to be okay. Hugh Newman may be the father of your child, but there is another man who will love you and your baby the way you deserve to be loved. And that's not all."

"Oh, yes it is," Bia said, backing away.

"Your family cares about you deeply and will rally around you during your pregnancy. You have absolutely nothing to fear."

Okay, this is the last straw. Who does this woman think she is bringing my family into this, as she spouts her woo-woo nonsense pretending like she knows what's going on? She obviously has no idea what she's talking about.

But if so, how did she know Bia was pregnant and that Hugh was the father? Conjecture? A lucky guess?

"This is none of your business," Bia said. "I'd appreciate it if you'd stop with the advice."

Maya's face turned scarlet. As Bia passed through

the curtains into the front of the shop, Maya said, "Bia, I'm sorry. I would never say or do anything to hurt you. Not on purpose."

Bia stopped and whirled around, looking Maya in the eyes. "Hurt me? You don't even know me. So please stop talking like you do. Stay out of my business, okay? Stay out of mine, and I will certainly stay out of yours."

Chapter Two

"I'm pregnant, Aiden."

Aiden Woods sat at Bia's kitchen table across from her, weighing his words before he spoke. He was inclined to make a joke—something about not being ready to be a father or that pregnancy was impossible since they'd never had sex.

Ha-ha?

Nope. Not funny.

For once in his life the filter of good sense kicked in before he stuck his foot in his mouth. Besides, one look at Bia's ashen face told him she wasn't joking.

"B?"

She didn't sleep around. So he had a pretty good idea who the father was. *Hugh Newman, the bastard.*

He wouldn't wish the guy on anyone, much less some-one he cared about.

"Are you sure?" The question sounded absurd to his own ears. But what else was he supposed to say? *I'm sorry? Tough break? Princess, I tried to warn you that Hugh Newman was a horse's ass with a pretty face, but did you listen? No, you didn't.*

"Yes, I'm quite sure. Three pregnancy tests don't lie." Her eyes welled up with tears.

Damn. Not the tears. Aiden fumbled for a minute. Then he reached across the table and took her hand. As the waterworks began to roll, she held on like he was her life preserver.

"God, I am so stupid, Aiden. How could I have gotten myself into this mess? How could I have let this happen?"

"Hey, hey, it's going to be okay." He got up and went around to her side of the table and slid onto the built-in banquette, putting his arm around her. She cried on his shoulder for a solid five minutes.

When Bia had called him at nine-thirty that morn-ing asking if he was free, if he could get away because she needed to talk to him about something important, he'd left the taping of *Catering to Dallas,* the reality television show that he produced, in the capable hands of the show's director, Miles Mercer, and met Bia. No wonder she hadn't wanted to meet him for coffee at the diner as he'd initially suggested. She wasn't a drama queen, so when she'd asked—and Bia never asked, not something like this—he knew it was important, but he'd never imagined a bomb like this.

Damn.

"Does Hugh know?" he asked, handing her a paper napkin from the holder on the table.

Bia wiped her eyes.

"No. You're the only person I've told. Well, you know and Maya LeBlanc *guessed*."

"Who is Maya LeBlanc?"

"She owns the new chocolate shop that's opening downtown. When I interviewed her yesterday, she took one look at me and asked me if I was pregnant."

Aiden squinted at her. "How the hell did she guess something like that?"

"I wasn't feeling well. I had a sinking spell and almost passed out. She must've put two and two together. Really, it wasn't such a stretch. Kind of personal of her to ask, but she did. Of course, that was after we'd been talking about her being highly intuitive. Maybe she was trying to prove a point about her intuition. I don't know."

"Did she guess who the father is?"

Bia flinched. "Absolutely not." She wrung her hands. "Well, sort of. But I didn't confirm that she was right. Come to think of it, though, I didn't even confirm that I was pregnant."

"But she knew it was Hugh? What is this woman, psychic or something?"

Bia inclined her head to the side and pierced him with impatient eyes. "If you think about it, after all the press Hugh and I got, that isn't such a stretch."

"Is she the one who tipped off the press back in March?"

Bia blinked. "Maya? I can't imagine that she would

do something like that. I mean, what would she stand to gain?"

Aiden shrugged. "*Someone* tipped them off. We don't know who. It sure seems like she's fishing."

"Well, if the press finds out that I'm pregnant, we'll know who told them."

Aiden nodded. "When are you going to tell Hugh?"

Bia took a deep breath, held it for a minute and then let it out audibly. She propped her elbow on the table and rested her forehead in her palms.

"You're going to tell him, aren't you?"

She didn't look up.

"Bia, you have to tell him."

"I don't *have* to do anything, Aiden. I can't even think right now. My head feels like it is about to explode."

"I understand," Aiden said. "But he's the father. He deserves to know."

She gave a little growl. "I didn't ask you to come here to lecture me."

That was his cue to back off. A woman he'd gone out with a couple of times had told him that sometimes women didn't want men to solve their problems; they just wanted them to listen. Seemed kind of ridiculous when a perfectly good solution to the problem was right there in front of them.

"I get that, but come on, B. If I got a woman pregnant, I'd want to know. It's as much his child as it is yours."

She rolled her eyes, which looked emerald green through the tears.

"You and Hugh Newman are two completely dif-

ferent animals, Aiden. I didn't tell you this, but—"
She grimaced and shook her head as if she could take
back the bait.

"You didn't tell me what?"

She grabbed another napkin and blew her nose.
"This is so embarrassing…." She closed her eyes for
a moment, as if gathering her courage. "In the midst
of the media frenzy, when the press was going crazy,
making me out to be some sort of mystery girlfriend,
Hugh's people offered to pay me to keep quiet."

Aiden shrugged. "That's not so out of character
for him."

"No, you don't get it. *He* didn't call me. He had his
people do it. Somehow, I don't think he will be very
happy to hear from me now."

Aiden balled his fists. He'd worked with the guy
years ago when he was in Hollywood. Aiden had been
a production assistant on one of his movies in the
early days. The guy was a jackass, out for no one but
himself.

"Well, if you call him and he ignores you, you've
done your duty. Once you let him know, it's off your
shoulders. But, B, if he wants to be part of the baby's
life, you have to let him. A kid can change a guy. Give
him a chance. If he wants nothing to do with the baby,
you're free to walk away."

He couldn't believe he was defending Hugh Newman.

"God, you're bossy," she said through a fresh
stream of tears.

"But you know I'm right."

She nodded. Then squeezed her eyes shut as she put her head on his shoulder and sobbed again.

"Hey, it's not that bad. I'm here for you. I know it's a shock, but you're strong. You can do this."

Once again, he slid his arm around her shoulder and she nestled into him as if she belonged there. His heart twisted, but he ignored it and lowered his head so that it rested on hers. Her hair smelled like coconut and something floral that made him breathe in a little deeper.

They stayed like that for a few minutes, until she pulled away. She reached for another napkin, wiped her eyes and blew her nose again. "You're right. I have to call him. The sooner I do it, the sooner it's over."

But she just sat there and didn't get up to get her phone.

"You have his number, right?"

She nodded. "Well, I have *a* number for him. I haven't talked to him in two months, since everything erupted. You know, it's funny, the other day I almost deleted his number, but I didn't."

"Why not? Were you harboring hopes of a second chance?"

She made a disgusted *tsking* sound and gave his arm a little shove. "Hardly. I didn't delete it because I got tied up with something else. I've been too busy at the paper since then to give him a second thought. I certainly haven't been pining over him, Aiden."

"Good to know," he said.

"Why is that good to know?"

"Because I don't want to see you get hurt again, B. I mean, you have to let him know about the child, but

I don't want you to harbor any expectations. I don't want you to get hurt."

"He *didn't* hurt me."

He studied her for a minute, doing his best to read her, but she'd put the wall up. She was good at that, shutting out people and situations so that they didn't get under her skin. This was only the second time he'd seen her cry. The other time was when she'd broken up with Duane. He would've held her then, too, but she'd blamed him for hiring the stripper that Duane had slept with two nights before their wedding. It took some time for their friendship to heal, but she'd finally acknowledged that if it hadn't happened then, it would've likely been someone else. Better to find out before the wedding than after they'd been married for a few years.

Aiden hated that he'd played a part in anything that had hurt Bia. But he knew Duane didn't love her the way she deserved to be loved. He had made his decision and he'd suffered the consequences.

"What do you think Hugh will say when I tell him?" she asked, her voice sounding unusually small.

That was a no-win question. The Hugh he knew was probably the last person who wanted a kid, especially with someone who couldn't advance his career. Bia was salt of the earth, the tenacious girl-next-door type. A woman any normal guy would fall over himself to be with. She was smart, funny and loyal to those she cared about. And he'd realized too late that he'd loved her all his life.

"I think what's more important is what you're going

to say. How you pose it to him sets the tone for his response."

She opened her mouth but closed it again, sitting back against the banquette and sighing. "I don't know what to say." She threw up her hands and let them fall into her lap.

"Tell him the truth. Cut-and-dry."

"Hi, Hugh. It's Bia Anderson. Remember me? No? Well, I was your Celebration, Texas, tour guide. Yeah, right, that one. The one your people offered to pay to be quiet. Funny thing, I'm pregnant. Yeah, that's right. You and I are going to be parents. Isn't that great news? I'm sure that's changed your mind about me—makes me so much more attractive, doesn't it?"

She rolled her eyes. "I've got nothing, Aiden."

He didn't know what to say. Usually, Bia had no problem saying what was on her mind. That's what made her a good reporter and had gotten her the top job at the paper. It was a rare circumstance that she was hesitant to make a call or speak her mind.

Of course Bia didn't know what to say. She didn't play contrived Hollywood games, which was one of the many things that Aiden loved about her. It was why this was so hard for her.

"Let's think about this," he said. "He'll probably be shocked. Be prepared for that. He might need some time to digest things before he's able to wrap his mind around it."

Bia chewed her thumbnail.

"And there's always Kristin. If he's really in love with her, this is going to make things pretty rocky for them. If he told her the tour guide story, she'll probably be pretty upset."

Bia snorted. "Heaven forbid we upset Kristin Capistrano."

Aiden held up his hands. "Hey, I'm just trying to help."

"I know you are. I'm sorry."

"There's always the possibility that they're not in love," he offered. "At least not with each other. They're filming a movie together in a few weeks. The relationship is good press. Just watch. But be prepared. He may want to keep things quiet about the baby until after the premiere. Don't be surprised."

Bia blanched. "That could be a year."

Aiden touched her arm. It was warm and soft. Her skin broke out into goose flesh on contact. He tried not to read anything into that. Instead, he reminded himself that she was pregnant. With another man's child. Somehow, that just made him feel more protective of her.

"But if he's any sort of human being, he will man-up in due time."

They sat quietly for a moment. The only sound in the kitchen was the hum of the refrigerator and the faint tick of the old-fashioned red enamel rooster clock that hung over the banquette.

"I know I've already told you this, but my dad did a great job raising me. Still, I always felt as if I were missing out because I didn't have *two* parents. A kid deserves *two* parents."

"You're preaching to the choir," Aiden said. "Your dad was more of a father to me than my own."

Aiden's dad had left the family when Aiden was nine years old. The age where every boy needs a father figure most. Aiden had spent more time at the Andersons' house hanging out with Bia's dad, Hank, than at his own. Hank had taught him how to throw a football, taken him fishing and taught him how to drive a car with a manual transmission.

"If Hugh wants to be part of the baby's life—or even better, if he wants to make a life with us—I'd be willing to consider it."

Aiden had to grit his teeth to keep from telling her not to count on it. Because Aiden knew if he said it, he'd be the bad guy. The jerk. No, he'd just keep quiet and let Hugh speak for himself. Maybe the guy would surprise everyone. Fat chance, but stranger things had happened.

"So, you'd be willing to make that sacrifice, huh? Living with the sexiest man alive? Wow, you're such a martyr, Princess. Such a martyr."

She rolled her eyes at him. Then she nestled into the crook between his arm and shoulder, that place where she fit so well.

"What's next, after you call Hugh?"

"I have a doctor's appointment Thursday."

"What time?"

"Why?"

"I'll go with you."

"You don't have to do that, Aiden."

"I know, but I want to. I'll be there for you, for moral support.

Cell phone in hand, Bia went into the bedroom and shut the door. Aiden was waiting in the kitchen. He'd said he understood that she needed to be alone when she made the call.

She wondered if he was standing guard, making sure she actually went through with it. She eyed the window, contemplating crawling out of it. But she knew that although she might be able to run away now, she'd never be able to escape the truth. She might as well make the call while Aiden was there. Besides, he would know if she chickened out. He had this uncanny way of reading her.

After what had happened with Maya yesterday, she wondered if she was too much of an open book or too transparent, but that had never been the case before. In fact, if anything, most people accused her of being too closed, too prickly. Maya's correct guess that Bia was pregnant had been a fluke. That's all there was to it. She would just need to make sure Maya didn't say anything to anyone else. She would go talk to her again later that week.

But right now, first things first. She needed to make the call.

Her hand was shaking as she picked up the phone and pulled up Hugh's number in her contacts. She wanted to laugh at the irony—how many women would pay to have Hugh Newman's private number, to hear his voice over the line? But this was a call that she dreaded more than any she'd ever placed.

She stared at her phone screen for a moment, at the ten-digit number and the small thumbnail photo of Hugh's face in the top left-hand corner of the page.

Her finger hovered over the call button, but she was paralyzed. She couldn't press it.

Maybe she should send him a certified letter?

Right.

That was the big chicken's way out. She didn't know what address to send it to, and, even if she did, she had no guarantee he would be the one to open it—certified letter or not. The rules that applied to the little people didn't always hold true for people like Hugh and his set.

"Oh, for God's sake," she muttered under her breath. "Just call and get it over with."

Her shaking finger came down hard on the call button. She held the phone to her ear before she could change her mind. For a few seconds, there was no sound and she was just about ready to pull the phone back and make sure she'd actually dialed the number. But before she could, she heard the ring, distant and tinny.

Bia paced the length of the room as the phone rang…four times before an automated attendant picked up. A generic, robotic voice informed her, "The person at this number is not available. Please leave your name and number after the tone."

Not even a promise that the person would call back at his convenience. But the one thing that robo-attendant did get right was that Hugh was not available—not physically or emotionally.

Bia hung up. No way was she going to leave such a personal message on his voice mail. For that matter, she didn't even know if the number still belonged to him.

She slumped down on the bed and stared at the phone's flat black screen.

Now what?

She should've known that he wouldn't pick up. Why would he? It wasn't as if he'd been waiting for her to call. She half expected to get a call back from his assistant, the one who had offered to pay her off—

That gave her an idea.

She brought up her call log and scrolled through it. Sure enough, there was the assistant's California number. What if she called him and asked him to have Hugh call her back? That it was a matter of great importance... Yeah, but there was no way she would make it past the guard dog without revealing what the call was about.

Wait a minute.... She stood up. Recently the paper had run a story on a phone app that manufactured *disposable* cell phone numbers, but for the life of her she couldn't remember the name of the company. She hadn't written the story. She'd edited it and probably seventy-five other articles since then. Still, she knew how she could find it. She called up the phone's browser and typed "how to disguise your cell number." The first link at the top of the list was for the company the paper had profiled.

She downloaded the app, got a disposable number with a California area code and dialed Hugh again.

Miracle of miracles, he picked up on the second ring.

"Hugh Newman."

It was now or never.

"Hugh, this is Bia Anderson. From Celebration, Texas."

There was complete silence on the other end of the line.

"Please don't hang up. I don't want anything from you, but I do have to tell you that I'm pregnant and you're the father."

She heard him exhale. At least he was still there. He'd gotten the message.

"This is a bad time." His voice was heavy with annoyance. "I'll call you back."

Chapter Three

The message was waiting for Maya when she logged into the Facebook page she had set up for Maya's Chocolates.

Hello, Maya! I'm so happy to learn that you are opening a shop in the United States. I had the pleasure of tasting your chocolate almost thirty years ago when I was in St. Michel. And sure if it hasn't been haunting me ever since. I will be in the Dallas area next week and I will stop in and say hello. Charles Jordan

While she wasn't inundated with fan mail, she did get a piece now and again. There was nothing out of the ordinary about the message. Except for the line, *And sure if it hasn't been haunting me ever since.*

Something about the turn of those words had been haunting *her*.

They called to mind a man she had known long ago. Actually, it was about twenty-nine or thirty years ago that Ian had been in her life. *Huh.* Another coincidence. But he'd disappeared just as fast as he'd appeared and swept her off her feet.

The memory weighed heavily on her heart.

Maya clicked on Charles Jordan's name, eager to see if she could find any more information on his profile page. But he didn't have a photo of himself for his profile picture. Instead, he had a generic picture of a snowcapped mountain range.

The page had been created a couple of years ago, but there hadn't been much activity. There were no other pictures and his list of friends was not open for the public to view.

Maya grappled with an uneasy feeling. Mr. Jordan's words, *And sure if it hasn't been haunting me ever since,* rang in her mind. In her head, she'd heard them in Ian's voice. They were as clear as if he'd spoken them an hour ago.

Ian Brannigan. Her Irishman. Her love.

He'd simply left one day, never called and never come back. For a long time, she had been so numb she could barely function. Then she had gotten angry. That's when she'd called his family in Dublin for contact information. Even though several years had passed by that point, Maya had been ready for an explanation. That's when the real heartbreak started. His mother had delivered the sad news that Ian was dead. He'd died in an accident on his way home from France.

That's why he'd never called. That's why the future she'd hoped they would have together never happened. That's why she'd never been able to fall in love with anyone else.

Ian had taken the largest part of her heart with him on that cold October day. And the rest of it had died nine months later when the nurse took their baby girl from her arms and whisked her away.

She was barely eighteen years old. She wasn't married, and the baby's father had obviously abandoned them. Or at least that's what everyone had thought then. But he hadn't abandoned them. It was both crushing and vindicating to learn that Ian hadn't abandoned them. He hadn't even known that she was carrying his child when he'd kissed her goodbye that last time.

However, that didn't change the fact that Maya was an unwed teenage mother, a disgrace to her family.

Her mother and grandmother made arrangements for her to go away for a while. She was allowed to come back after the baby was born. That way no one would ever be the wiser, the family name would be saved and they could hold their heads up high.

Maya knew that she could hope all she wanted to, but this Charles Jordan, no matter the imagined similarities, was not her Ian Brannigan.

Once again, Maya clicked on the message balloon icon and reread Charles Jordan's message. She was just about to type a quick reply when she heard a knock at the front door.

She wasn't expecting anyone, but she made her way

from the kitchen to the front of the store to see who was calling. To her surprise, it was Bia.

Things had ended on such a horrific note the other day that Maya quite honestly thought it would be a very long time before she heard from Bia again.

She gave a friendly wave to test the waters. To her relief, Bia waved back, even if she wasn't smiling. The wave had to be a good sign. At least she hoped it was. She would find out soon enough, she thought, as she opened the door and greeted Bia with the warmest American greeting she could muster. She didn't give her the customary French greeting, a kiss on each cheek. She had a feeling she needed to tread lightly.

"Hello!" Maya said. "I am so happy to see you. I wasn't expecting you after what happened yesterday. I'm so sorry, Bia. But I'm so glad you've come back."

Interesting, Maya pondered. *First, I'm thinking of Ian, and now Bia shows up. Perhaps the universe is trying to tell me something.*

But given this second chance and how easily Bia was frightened off yesterday, Maya was determined to take things slowly. She would build the relationship before she broke the news.

"I'm sorry I overreacted yesterday," Bia said. "But I have to ask—and I need an honest answer—how did you know I'm pregnant?"

Maya shrugged. "Intuition, I suppose."

"So, it was a lucky guess," Bia replied.

"If that's what you would prefer to call it. Shall we go into the kitchen where we can sit down and talk?

I'll make you a cup of hot chocolate. You need your calcium."

Bia held her ground. "First, I need your word that you will not tell a soul about this. If you think the media went crazy when they thought Hugh and I were seeing each other, this will blow up in both of our faces. Especially after he lied about the nature of our... *acquaintance*."

Maya's brow creased in a look of what seemed to be genuine concern. "Of course you have my word. This is a very private matter. I want you to know that I am here for you. I promise I will not do anything to put you or your baby in emotional jeopardy."

"I need to ask you something, and, again, you must give me an honest answer."

Maya nodded. "Please. Anything."

"Have you ever said anything to the press about my previous relationship with Hugh Newman?"

Maya recoiled and looked genuinely shocked by the question. A good sign, as far as Bia was concerned. Still, she had to look Maya in the eyes as she asked. Just as Maya had a sixth sense about people, Bia could intuit when people were lying. Bia's gut was telling her that Maya was telling the truth.

Maya put her right hand over her heart. "I swear to you. I have not said one word. I did see the two of you together at the Doctor's Ball, but I would never gossip about you. I would swear this on my mother's and grandmother's graves."

"Thank you, Maya. I believe you. And I believe that you will keep your word about not talking to a soul other than me about my current situation."

Maya held up her right hand. "I solemnly swear. Now, let's have some hot chocolate. Yes?"

Maya's version of hot chocolate was like nothing Bia had ever tasted before. It was nearly as thick as melted chocolate and tasted so good it curled Bia's toes.

Le chocolat chaud, Maya called it.

Bia called it divine. She had to pace herself to keep from gulping it. To that end, she tried to employ some of the tasting principles that Maya had taught her yesterday. She sipped the drink and let the warm liquid flow over her tongue.

"Umm, is that cinnamon I taste?"

Maya nodded.

"There's something else I can't quite identify…." Bia closed her eyes and rolled the liquid around on her palate.

"I added a tiny dash of cayenne and a few flecks of *fleur de sel.*"

"Salt and pepper," Bia noted wryly.

Maya laughed her laugh that seemed to set Bia at ease, and the world seemed a little brighter. Bia didn't have many close girlfriends. She'd always related better to guys. She simply didn't enjoy the drama that always seemed to go hand in hand with women. On occasion, Bia had been accused of being too direct— one of the qualities that made her a good reporter, of course. But Maya hadn't been offended by Bia's head-on approach. Come to think of it, Maya had been pretty direct herself yesterday.

At least they understood each other.

"Have you had a chance to think about what you're going to do?" Maya asked.

"About?"

"The baby, of course."

"I'm having this baby. I'm twenty-eight years old. I can handle it. I was adopted. Actually, I just found out a few months ago, just before my adoptive father passed away. I had a good childhood despite my adoptive mother dying when I was five. Her husband—my father—never remarried. So, essentially, I grew up without a mother. My father was very good to me, but I can't help but wonder lately why my birth mother didn't want me. I have no information about her. I'm not sure whether I should go digging or not."

"I'm sure she would be thrilled to connect with you," Maya said. "At least you'll never know until you try."

"What? Is that your intuition speaking? I can't be *sure* that she would be thrilled. I mean, she gave me up. For all I know, she might have a family of her own. They might not know about me. I might be that unwelcome surprise from her past popping up at the most inopportune time."

"But you can't be certain of that, either. For all you know, you could be missing out on a second chance at family."

Bia shrugged. "But there's no way to know that for certain."

"There's no way to know that you won't walk out of here and get hit by a car, but the likelihood of disaster is slim. What I'm saying is, if you are open to having your birth mother in your life— Are you?"

Bia nodded.

"Good, then keep an open mind. I think it would be especially important to meet her now that you have a little one on the way. For that matter, have you talked to the father?"

Bia grimaced. "I spoke to Hugh briefly. Told him the situation. He told me it wasn't a good time to talk and that he would call me back. But he hasn't. I don't really expect him to."

Thoughtfully, Maya ran her finger around the rim of her demitasse cup. "At the risk of—how do you say it—sticking my nose in where it doesn't belong? Hugh Newman may be the father of your child, but he is not the right man for you."

"Story of my life," Bia murmured.

"Make no mistake, there is someone out there for you. He is already in your life. You simply must learn to see what is right in front of you."

Thursday afternoon, Aiden was leaning against his car, which was parked in the lot of Bia's doctor, waiting for her to arrive.

When she finally did, she got out of her car and said, "Aiden, you're here? I told you not to come."

Her words said one thing, but the way she said them confirmed that he'd been right to not let her face her first doctor's appointment alone.

"I thought you might want some moral support."

She smiled. "I'm a big girl, Aiden. I can handle this." Then she hugged him and whispered, "Thanks for being here. I don't know what I'd do without you."

He put his arm around her as they walked from the

parking lot into the lobby. To the untrained eye, they probably looked like a happy couple eager to get the lowdown on their first child. He could play that role, especially if Hugh wasn't going to.

"Have you heard from Hugh?"

She stiffened, pulled away ever so slightly. "No. But he knows. And he knows how to reach me and where to find me."

"Ball's in his court, then," Aiden said as he opened the office door and stood back so Bia could enter.

Two other women, both obviously further along in their pregnancies than Bia, waited. Both had men with them, and Aiden was instantly reassured that he'd made the right decision to come along. No doubt Bia would've soldiered through on her own, but she shouldn't have to face this alone.

"I'm going to go sign in," she said. "Go ahead and sit down and I'll be right back…with mountains of paperwork, no doubt."

He sat down in a chair across from one of the couples. The woman looked as if she were smuggling a basketball under her dress. Aiden looked away, trying to imagine what Bia would look like that far along. She'd be gorgeous.

"Is this your first child?" the woman asked.

"Uhh…" Obviously, she'd caught him staring. But she didn't seem annoyed or put off. Her husband was reading the newspaper and didn't seem to notice that Aiden had been scoping out his wife's belly. Good thing.

Rather than dive headlong into an explanation, he simply said, "Yes. It is." After all, he hadn't been party to another pregnancy before. She hadn't asked him if he was the father.

"Congratulations to you and your wife." She beamed at him and clasped her hands over her belly. "You have some exciting months ahead of you. Years actually. Kids will change your life."

Yep. So I've heard.

He nodded. Pondering the thought of Bia as his wife as she walked toward him, clipboard in hand. She stirred in him a feeling that was equal parts primal lust and Cro-Magnon protective. He'd always been attracted to her. Hell, if he were honest with himself, he'd admit that he'd always been in love with Bia Anderson.

He just hadn't been able to admit it to himself until his roommate Duane had taken an interest in her at that party their freshman year of college. He couldn't remember who threw the party or what the occasion was, but he would never forget what she looked like standing there kissing Duane. At that moment, something inside him shifted and snapped into place. By the time he finally woke up and realized what had been under his nose all his life, she was off-limits. So, Aiden had settled for a friendship because it was better to have her in his life under restricted terms than not at all.

Duane never had treated her right. He used to think Aiden was joking when he said things like, "Too bad you saw her first, man," and "If you don't treat her right, I'm going to take her away from you." They would all laugh and then Aiden would try to get interested in some other girl. Inevitably, those relationships never worked out. Bia thought he was the world's biggest player. And he would laugh it off and say, "None of them compare to you."

And she thought he was joking.

He'd come here, taken the *Catering to Dallas* gig, to be near her. Things had been going well between them. The best way to describe them was platonic with chemistry. They were solid, and he wanted to take things slowly, let the relationship develop naturally. And then Hugh Newman came to town, proving it had been a dumb idea to take things slowly. It had been a grave miscalculation to not move at the speed of Hugh.

As Bia sat down in the chair next to him, the nurse called back the woman who had been talking to him—Sandra something…he hadn't caught her last name.

"Good luck, you two," she said as she and her husband walked toward the waiting nurse. "This truly is the beginning of the happiest time of your lives."

"Thanks," he said. "Nice talking to you."

"Making friends, already?" Bia murmured. "You are such a flirt."

"I wasn't flirting," he said. "I was just being cordial. They think we're married."

Bia rolled her eyes at him. "Obviously they don't know who they're dealing with. You, with your commitment allergy. I'm surprised that you didn't run screaming for the door after she said that."

"That hurts, B. Like a stab right through the heart. You know I'm committed to you. You're the only woman in the world for me."

She made a *tsking* sound and gave his arm a little shove and muttered, "Spare me." Then she refocused on her paperwork, but she was smiling as she wrote. He noticed that she had left the spot on the form that asked for the name of the child's father blank. He thought about asking her what, if anything, she was going to tell the doctor, but he decided to wait until after the appointment.

"Obviously, we make a good couple," he said. "We fooled them."

"Yeah, well, welcome to the grand illusion. When a man and a woman come to an OB-GYN office together, they're usually involved. We just happen to be part of the slim minority who aren't."

"We should stop pretending and get married, Bia."

She didn't look up from her paperwork, but she laughed. "Says he who is allergic to monogamy. Don't joke about marriage, Aiden. Some things are sacred."

"Who says I'm joking?"

This time she pierced him with an exasperated look. "Settle down and quit distracting me. I have to finish filling out this paperwork before they call me back." She started writing again. "Besides, you don't have a ring. You can't propose to a woman without a ring."

He pretended to pat down his pockets, looking for a ring. "Touché. You got me there."

She did have him. Heart and soul. He'd never realized just how deep his feelings for her ran until recently. If only he could tell her without the comedy routine. Easier said than done.

A few minutes later, the nurse called Bia back.

Aiden followed her to the door. "I haven't finished my paperwork," she said.

"That's not a problem," the nurse said. "Maybe your husband could finish filling it out for you while we're getting you ready to see the doctor?"

"He's not my husband," Bia said.

The nurse smiled, and she looked from Bia to Aiden. "Well, okay. Do you want him to come back with you?"

She asked the question as if he would be entering a restricted-access area.

"Oh…" Bia glanced at Aiden and then back to the nurse. "I guess he can wait out here. Would you mind, Aiden?"

"Probably a good idea." The nurse smiled at him and took a step closer. "The first visit is always the longest. The doctor will want to go over the genetic history of your family and that of the baby's father. It will take a while, but if you'd like to wait, let's get you something to drink—would you like coffee? A soda?"

He felt Bia pull away from him emotionally. She had a strange look on her face, and he wasn't sure why. Probably just nerves. This was suddenly becoming very real, and she wanted to go back there alone.

"Aiden, I'm fine. Why don't you go back to work? There's no sense in you waiting."

"I don't mind. You might need me."

She softened, but the wall was still in place. That same wall that kept him a safe, platonic distance away. "It was so sweet of you to come. But really, I'm fine. Please go."

* * *

The nurse left Bia standing there while she fetched coffee for Aiden.

How utterly unprofessional. If the woman hadn't been wielding needles—once she'd made sure Aiden was comfortable—Bia might have schooled her on the meaning of a proper time and a place for everything. When a woman was walking through the door for her first obstetric appointment, it definitely *wasn't* the time or the place for the nurse to flirt with the man who had accompanied the pregnant woman. Just because he wasn't her husband didn't mean he was fair game.

Aiden seemed absolutely clueless to the effect he had on women. Sometimes she wondered if that cluelessness was more a case of playing dumb like a fox. *I'll be so disarmingly charming and oblivious to how gorgeous I am and see how many women I can lure in.*

He did it all the time, whether he was cognizant of it or not, and it made Bia crazy. He dated women long enough for them to fall for him and then he got the heck out of Dodge.

Since college, Bia had witnessed the never-ending parade of bimbos who were crazy for him. In fact, Bia was willing to wager that Aiden could give Hugh a run for the number of women he was stringing along.

The nurse, for example. The pregnant woman in the lobby... Well, that probably wasn't the same thing. She looked like she was about to pop and her husband was sitting right there. Still, the pregnant one could be filed in a subcategory of looking but not touching, which was fine.... Actually, it all was fine. She had no claim on him.

Since Aiden had moved to Celebration to work on *Catering to Dallas,* there hadn't been as many women. But he hadn't been there that long, and work kept him pretty busy. What little free time he had, he tended to spend with Bia. She'd come to think of herself as his safe haven.

They'd been friends for so long that she prided herself on being the person with whom he could hang out without fear of her getting the wrong idea or coming back with expectations.

That's not to say that Bia didn't find him attractive. For God's sake, he was probably *the* sexiest man she'd ever met. Sexier than Hugh Newman, hands-down sexier than Duane. A big part of what made him sexy to her was that she knew all the facets of Aiden. She'd seen the soul behind the one-hundred-watt smile and the smoldering I-want-you-now glances.

If there wasn't so much history between them, so much water under the bridge, he probably would've had her flat on her back a long time ago—and much faster than Hugh Newman. The difference was Hugh hadn't mattered.

A piece of her soul would die if she lost Aiden.

They hadn't gotten to this point overnight. The wine of their friendship had been maturing for years. And it had withstood nearly insurmountable mishaps.

When she'd found out Duane had slept with the stripper that Aiden had hired, she'd blamed Aiden. She had called off the wedding and sent Duane packing, but she blamed Aiden for enabling his friend. *Two nights before the wedding. Two nights.*

She'd had to cancel everything: the church, the caterer, the guests, the wedding hall. Her father had lost a good fifteen grand thanks to one night of someone else's utter stupidity.

The only reason she and Aiden were still talking today—and were as close as they'd become—was because Aiden had proven that Duane's actions had hurt him almost as much as they'd hurt Bia. Aiden had cut ties with Duane, but he hadn't left Bia alone until she'd accepted his apology. Once they'd cleared that hurdle, Aiden had never left. But they'd also agreed to never talk about the Duane–stripper fiasco again.

There had been a couple of times when Bia had been tempted to test the bounds of their friendship…to quench her curiosity about how his lips would taste… or how his hands would feel on her body…how he would feel inside her body.

She shivered at the thought and pulled the paper gown closed at her neck. But he was her friend. She shouldn't even go there mentally. Especially when she was sitting in a doctor's office pregnant with another man's child.

She took a deep breath and exhaled away the inappropriate thoughts about her friend. Her *friend*.

Even if she wouldn't allow herself to cross the line with Aiden, she was allowed to resent Nurse Flirty for so brazenly flirting with him. *Yeah, honey, you may pack a scary syringe, but if you want to get to him, you've gotta go through me.*

Finally, the doctor knocked on the door. He entered

the room, accompanied by—*oh, joy*—Nurse Flirty, who immediately turned her back on Bia and busied herself at the counter on the far wall.

"Hello, Ms. Anderson," said Dr. Porter. "It's nice to meet you."

He washed his hands and then shook Bia's hand before picking up her file.

"This is your first pregnancy?" he asked.

"It is," she said.

"I notice you left the space on the form for the father's name blank. Would you mind telling me why?"

Well, yes, she minded. She really didn't want to talk about him.

"He may or may not want to be a part of the child's life," Bia said. "That remains to be seen. So, until I know, I would prefer to leave him out of it."

The doctor rubbed his chin. "Regardless of whether or not he is part of the child's life, the baby will have his genes. It's important that we know as much about him as possible for your child's health. I'd prefer for his name to be part of the records."

A slow burn started in the pit of Bia's stomach. Maybe it was hormones; maybe it was this particular doctor's office. She'd chosen it because it was close rather than trekking all the way to Dallas for her checkups, which, according to everything she'd read, would be much more frequent than her annual checkup. She might need to rethink this decision since she wasn't feeling very comfortable.

"Dr. Porter, the baby's father is prominent, a celebrity who isn't local, and all communication thus far indicates that he doesn't want to be part of the child's life. I will do my due diligence and gather his medical history, but I'd like to keep his name out of the official records."

Bia noticed that the nurse was now facing her, unapologetically taking in every word of their conversation. Bia frowned at her, and she turned back around.

"Well…it's not optimal," Dr. Porter said. "But as you wish."

There was a knock at the door and another nurse stuck her head in. "Excuse me, Dr. Porter. May I see you for a moment? I'm sorry to interrupt, but there's an important matter."

"Certainly." He looked irritated, but he said, "Excuse me, Ms. Anderson. I'll be right back."

When the door had closed, the nurse turned back around to Bia. "I'm sorry—I just have to ask. Is Hugh Newman the father?"

"I beg your pardon?" Bia said.

"Is Hugh Newman the father of your baby?"

"You've got to be kidding me." Bia said.

"It's just that I knew you looked familiar and when you said the baby's father was a celebrity, I remembered seeing you on *XYZ* with Hugh. He is such a hottie. I'm such a fan. Don't worry—I won't tell anyone. You know, with HIPAA laws and all, I could get into big trouble if I told anyone."

Was this some sort of joke? Was she being *punked* for one of those reality television shows? Because this was the most surreal doctor visit she'd ever experienced in her life.

First, Nurse Flirty all but gave her number to Aiden

and now she was prying into a subject that Bia had clearly stated was a closed subject.

"It is him, isn't it?" the nurse said.

"Umm...I have to go," Bia said, getting to her feet.

"Dr. Porter isn't finished with your appointment yet. He'll be right back."

"That's okay. I'll make other arrangements. I need to go back to work. Would you please step outside so I can get dressed?"

"I'll go find Dr. Porter for you. It will only take a moment. Please don't go anywhere."

However, in less than a minute, Bia was dressed and in the lobby, where Aiden was still sipping the cup of coffee Nurse Flirty had fetched him.

"That didn't take long," he said. "What's wrong?"

"I'm leaving," Bia said and quietly let herself out the front door before the reception staff realized what was happening. She would call later, but now she needed to get out of there and rethink her plan. She'd call her doctor in Dallas and make the trip if that's what it took to maintain her privacy. Actually, she wondered, was privacy a thing of the past post-Hugh?

"What is going on?" Aiden repeated once they were in the parking lot.

"This is obviously not the right doctor for me," she said. "I didn't want to name the baby's father and they took issue with it."

"I noticed you left it blank," Aiden said. "But shouldn't that be your call?"

"You'd think. Actually, the doctor accepted it. I made the mistake of saying that the father was a celebrity who didn't want to be involved, and after Dr. Porter left the room for a moment, your girlfriend asked me point-blank if the father was Hugh. And she kept pressing it. So, I walked out."

"My girlfriend?"

"The nurse who got you all tucked in with juice and cookies while I was waiting."

"She's not even my type."

"She's female. I thought that was your type."

"Are you jealous?"

Maybe a little. Bia looked away. "No. I'm irritated."

"I don't blame you." He reached out and touched her chin with his finger, gently turning her head so that she was looking at him. "I'd be mad, too. That was pretty audacious of her."

Bia glanced up at him. The way he was standing so close to her, with one hip braced against the car, touching her and gazing at her so intently, she actually thought for a delusional moment that he might lean in and kiss her.

Her gaze fell to his lips, and she was suddenly a little too warm. Given the way everything had been imploding around her, she knew better than to go… there. As tempting as it might have been. She obviously wasn't herself. She took a step back.

"I'll say. I'll call my doctor in Dallas tomorrow—"

Her phone rang.

Bia sighed as she fished it out of her purse, fully expecting the display to show Dr. Porter's number. She had no intention of answering, but when she pulled out her phone to silence it, a number with a California area code lit up the screen.

Chapter Four

Bia let the call go to voice mail and waited until she got home to pick up the message. She wasn't about to have this conversation with Hugh in a doctor's parking lot. Plus, there was a very good chance that Hugh hadn't placed the call himself because it wasn't his number. Or at least not the number where Bia had reached him.

She was right. The person who had left the message was a guy named Steve Luciano, Hugh's attorney. It stung down to the quick that Hugh couldn't even be bothered to call her back himself.

The slippery jerk. How could she have been such a poor judge of character to let herself get blinded by a handsome face and lines he'd probably used on dozens of women to get exactly what he wanted?

The first thing she did after she picked up Luciano's message was call the office and tell them that she was going to be back later than she'd expected.

Then she went into the kitchen and made herself a cup of tea. She had to get her head together. Obviously she wasn't thinking clearly. She'd blown up at Maya in the middle of their interview the other day. Today she'd walked out of a doctor's appointment. Normally, she was stronger than that. Strong enough to resist the need to put someone like Nurse Flirty in her place.

She didn't know whether to blame it on the hormones or if the unexpected pregnancy had completely knocked her for a loop. Either way, she had to get a grip on this situation. Ignoring it wasn't going to change it.

For Bia, a cup of tea was a soothing ritual. Boiling the water, measuring out the tea leaves, letting the brew steep—all the steps forced her to slow down and take a breath. She set out the bone china cup that had belonged to her grandmother, probably the one person other than Aiden who had understood her best. After her mother had died, Bia used to spend summers with her Grandma Dee. It was always a magical time. They would read books together and have tea parties.

Grandma Dee was the one who had taught her how to brew tea and how emotionally healing it could be. When she drank from her grandmother's teacup, it was almost as if she were having tea with her even though she'd been gone more than eight years now.

Once the tea was ready, Bia took her cup, a piece of the chocolate from the box that Maya had given her the other day and her phone out to the table on the redbrick patio area in the backyard. When she was settled, she debated whether or not she would even return Steve Luciano's call.

It didn't take a genius to figure out that Luciano had called to set the tone—to intimidate. Maybe even to scare her off so that the situation might magically disappear in a *poof* of second thoughts since the lawyer was involved.

Well, she didn't like this any more than Hugh did, but it wasn't going to go away. They had to deal with it. As Bia took a bite of chocolate—this piece tasted like it was infused with lavender—she let it melt on her tongue and then took a small sip of her Earl Grey and let the flavors mingle. By the time she'd finished the piece of chocolate, she felt a little more like herself.

It made her regret how she'd blown up at Maya the other day. Especially thinking about how Maya couldn't have been nicer when Bia had gone in the next day to talk to her. In the same spirit that she hadn't run away from that unpleasant situation, she needed to handle Hugh the right way, too. To do this right, she needed to start by calling back Mr. Steve Luciano.

She played his message. His voice had a no-nonsense tone with just a hint of intimidation. The message was pretty straightforward: "Hello, Ms. Anderson, this is Steve Luciano, legal representative for Mr. Newman. Would you please call me back at your earliest convenience?"

At my earliest convenience? How genteel.

She fortified herself with the last sip of tea, took a deep breath and hit Redial. When a receptionist picked up, it suddenly hit her that she might not be able to get him right on the line.

"Yes, hello, this is Bia Anderson returning Steve Luciano's call."

She hoped that they wouldn't have to play several rounds of telephone tag before they finally connected. Lord knew this wasn't a call Bia wanted to take at the office, but she certainly couldn't wait around the house for him to call her back. If he wasn't available, she'd tell him he had to call her back after seven o'clock.

"Yes, Ms. Anderson, Mr. Luciano is expecting your call. Please hold and I will put you right through."

Oh. Well…okay.

"Thank you," Bia said in her steadiest voice.

Luciano was on the line in less than thirty seconds. Bia imagined that might be a record.

"Hello, Ms. Anderson. Steve Luciano here. Thank you for calling me back."

Did I have a choice? "You're welcome."

"Let me start by saying that Mr. Newman is deeply concerned about this situation and he appreciates your discretion, that you kept this quiet. However, I must admit that I'm surprised you contacted Mr. Newman again since you refused our generous offer a couple of months ago. When I offered to pay you for your… tour guide services. Have you reconsidered my initial offer?"

Bia was a bit taken aback. "I haven't reconsidered anything, Mr. Luciano. I don't want his money. I'm pregnant. It was simply a courtesy call to Hugh to advise him of the situation. And it appears that he's handed me off to you."

"I see. As I said, please know that Mr. Newman appreciates your discretion in this matter. He asked me to convey that he wants nothing but the best for you and your child—"

"His child," Bia corrected.

"Of course, you must understand that we have no proof that he is, in fact, the father. Not that I'm doubting you, of course."

"Of course. I suppose you'll just have to take my word on it."

"I see. Mr. Newman is very busy right now—"

"As am I," Bia said. "So why don't we cut to the chase?"

"Of course."

Of course. I see. I see. Of course. It was all a bit grating.

"I suppose that would be where you come in," said Luciano. "Exactly how much do you need to make this problem disappear?"

Bia stood and began pacing. "Excuse me? What exactly are you suggesting?"

"I'm not suggesting anything."

"Listen, Mr. Luciano. The only reason I called was to do the decent thing and let Hugh know that he is going to be a father. I'm going to have this child. Surely you weren't suggesting otherwise."

"Of course not. But I am strongly advising that you think twice before you try to extort money out of Mr. Newman."

She stopped. "Wait just a minute. You were the one who asked me how much I needed to make this go away."

"Yes, Ms. Anderson. If you must know, you are not unique in your claim. Last year alone three women claimed they were carrying babies fathered by Mr. Newman."

The bastard. Is he out there scattering his seed across the land?

"I'm sorry to hear that. Whether he's the father or not, there are innocent children involved. Children who deserve parents who love them and did not choose to be in the middle of a battle."

Luciano was silent on the other end of the line. He was probably employing the "he who speaks first loses" tactic.

"Let me make this easy for you and Mr. Newman. All I want to know is whether he wants to be a part of this child's life or not."

"Ms. Anderson, as I said before, I can't answer that question until we have DNA proof that the child is in fact his."

"Then I'll take that as a *no*. Tell Mr. Newman he has nothing to worry about. I've done my duty with this phone call. As far as I'm concerned, he is waiving any and all parental rights. Tell him the baby and I will be perfectly fine without him."

When she hung up, a huge sob escaped her throat. Only then did she realize that tears were streaming down her cheeks. She sat at the patio table and put her head in her hands and sobbed. The tears weren't for herself, but for this child, who had not been conceived in love and had been rejected even before he or she had come into the world.

"That's not a very good start to life, little one," she whispered.

She sat up and wrapped her arms around her middle, protectively hugging her unborn child. She stayed like that until she'd shed the last tear.

Then it was almost as if a switch had flipped inside her. They would be fine. She and her baby would be perfectly fine on their own. This child may not have been conceived in love, but she would love the child enough for two parents. Sure, if she'd had the choice she would've brought a child into the world under different circumstances, but this was the hand they'd been dealt.

She would make darn sure that she made the most of it. As she sat there, looking at the trees and flowers in the yard, landscaping that her father had done—her father, a man who was no blood relation to her, a man who had raised her on his own in the name of all that was decent and kind and right. She suddenly realized that she was probably better off having been raised by someone who wanted her rather than resented by someone whose DNA she shared.

No doubt, it would be a challenge being a single parent, but she would pay forward what her father had done for her.

She was going to be a mother.

"I'm having a baby." She said the words aloud, letting the true meaning sink in and flow through her.

This baby would be loved and wanted and cherished.

Bia went into the office on Saturday to catch up. She didn't mind being there alone. In fact, she liked the peace and quiet. She could leave her door open and lose herself in her work—something she hadn't been able to do in ages.

After pouring herself a cup of coffee and turning on the television in her office to an all-news channel, she settled at her desk and turned down the volume on the TV with the remote so that she could barely hear it.

It was the best kind of company for a day like this—quiet when she needed to concentrate, yet she could look up and glimpse what was going on in the world when she wanted a quick break. Even though she loved to be in the thick of the newsroom hubbub, she loved the occasional day of solitude. Right now, with all that had been going on, it was especially good to have time to breathe, time to regroup and center herself.

She took out her notes for the business profile on Maya's Chocolates. She needed to write that story first and get it ready to go for the next edition. Amid all the craziness, she hadn't sent a photographer over to get a picture of Maya.

Good grief. She had to get her act together. Since she was going to be a mother, it wasn't going to get any easier than it was right now. The carefree days of thinking only of herself and her schedule were numbered. That was okay. It was part of this next chapter of her life. Her hand found her still-flat belly and rested there. She'd make it work.

She opened a fresh document on her computer and poised her fingers on the keyboard. Usually by now she would have composed the story lede; she would've written it in her head so that it flowed onto the page when she was ready to begin the article. But since interviewing Maya, she hadn't had a sane moment to rub two thoughts together, much less compose the first paragraph of a news story.

The history of the business was what immediately leaped out at Bia. The beauty of how it had been handed down through the generations—from mother to daughter to granddaughter seemed like a great way to start…maybe working in the imagery of the copper pots….

Bia's gaze focused on the TV as she moved words around in her head. There was so much happening on the screen. The ticker of news snippets below the anchor, the collection of small boxes highlighting the other stories—it all amounted to the visual equivalent of white noise: such an overload of info that none of it registered…until the ticker at the bottom changed to a breaking news alert that nearly made her heart stop. *Actor Hugh Newman dead at age thirty-five.*

Bia blinked at the screen, unsure if she'd read it right. She grabbed the remote and, with shaking hands, used the DVR control to pause the news program. She stood up at her desk so she could see the television better and rewound the show to the place where the breaking news alert had begun.

She pushed Play. Her vision became white and fuzzy around the edges as her fear was confirmed. Hugh was dead…car accident in the Hollywood Hills…alone in the car. No further details available at the moment….

* * *

Aiden's condo was less than a quarter mile from the paper's office.

"Are you home?" she asked.

Thank goodness he was.

In a fog, she grabbed her purse and keys, locked the office and set out on foot to go to the only person she could talk to about this.

Hugh wasn't exactly her favorite person these days, but she would've never wished something as tragic as this to happen to him. He was only thirty-five years old. He couldn't be dead. He should've had more than half his life ahead of him.

It was surreal. And cruel. Before she walked out of the building that housed the office, she stood with her arms crossed, digging her fingernails into the flesh of her arms, hoping to wake herself up. Desperately hoping and praying that this was all a bad dream and she would wake up and realize everything was fine.

She cut across the parking lot behind the office building. She noticed that the hose that had always seemed out of place in an office parking lot had unraveled and was leaking again. She'd have to tell her boss, Drew. He rarely came into the office during the week anymore, but sometimes he washed his car in the parking lot on weekends—despite how he could afford to take it to a professional to get it cleaned and detailed. He was that kind of hands-on guy, she thought as she walked through the grass that separated the lot from the sidewalk. She was doing her best to keep her mind on anything but the bombshell she'd just heard.

Hugh is dead.

Dead.

She felt as if she sort of floated along the path. She couldn't cry. She couldn't feel her legs, either. She reached up and swiped at her face to make sure the numbness that had overridden the rest of her body hadn't caused her to not feel the tears. But her face was dry.

She was on autopilot, driven by a force that she couldn't control. But she must not have been completely out of her mind, because about three quarters of the way to Aiden's place, she became cognizant of a car driving very slowly behind her. She glanced back at the nondescript white sedan. She didn't recognize it, and the way the sunlight was reflecting off the windshield, she couldn't make out the driver's features.

Celebration, Texas, was probably one of the safest places in the Southwest. She'd never been hesitant to get out and walk, and, in fact, if she had the choice to walk rather than drive, she walked. It really was her preferred mode of transportation. Still, it unnerved her to have this car poking along behind her.

The street leading to Aiden's house was two blocks off Main Street and mostly residential. There were people outside mowing lawns and washing cars; kids were playing ball in one of the yards across the street. If the person following her was up to no good, there would be plenty of witnesses and people to come to her aid.

Even so, when she got to the next driveway, she walked a few steps up the driveway toward the house and stopped, fishing her cell phone out of her purse. If the person was following her, he or she would ei-

ther stop, too—but she would be at a safe distance—
or would drive on by.

The car slowed to a stop at the foot of the driveway.
Bia quickly dialed Aiden's number. Maybe the person
was lost. Maybe he just needed directions.

The person sat in the idling car. A red pickup truck
pulled up behind the white car, honked and finally
zoomed around it.

"Hello?" Aiden's voice sounded on the other end
of the line. Still, the car sat there.

"Hey, it's me," Bia said. "Strange thing. A car's
been following me. I'm only about two houses away
from you. Would you mind coming outside just in case
I need some help?"

"Do you want to stay on the line with me or hang
up and call nine-one-one?"

Someone opened the passenger side of the white
car.

So, there was more than one person. Her heart thudded. So much for the earlier numbness. Her mind flit-
ted to Hugh and the tragedy, and she couldn't help
wonder if somehow this had something to do with
him. But what?

The person who got out of the passenger side of
the car was a small man who looked vaguely familiar.
The minute he said, "Bia Anderson"—it was more of
a statement than a question—she knew exactly who
had been tailing her.

It was the same scumbag who had hounded her
when the "woman in the blue sundress" scandal
started when Hugh had been in Celebration two
months earlier.

Oh, boy. As the guy aimed a small video camera at her, Bia knew what was coming next and she looked for an escape route.

"Hello, Bia. Joey Camps from *XYZ Celebrity News.* How ya doin' today?"

As Joey walked toward her with the camera, Bia glanced around. The only escape route was around the hedge and across the lawn. She turned her back and made her way to the opening in the shrubbery. She heard Joey's footsteps behind her.

"Oh, come on. Don't be that way. I just wanted to ask you to say a few words about Hugh Newman. Tragic loss, isn't it?"

Did the guy have no decency?

Bia knew she was being filmed, but she kept her head down and her sights set on making her way across the lawn to the opening in the hedge that would let her out onto the sidewalk.

"Nothing to say about your good friend? We're trying to put together a memorial segment for the show."

Bia knew that was a lie. They would probably use the uncut footage or maybe pair it with a clip of Kristin mourning Hugh's loss. Her heart ached for Kristin. She didn't want her to be left brokenhearted. Despite everything that had transpired, she hoped that Hugh had known true love with someone.

"Come on, Bia," Joey pressed. "Just give us one statement about Hugh Newman and we'll leave you alone."

"I barely knew Hugh. He was only in Celebration for five days. Still, I'm deeply saddened to learn of his accident. It's a tragic loss."

"But, yeah, weren't you like his girlfriend when he was here?"

"No. I was his...*tour guide*." She lifted her chin defiantly.

Joey snorted. "I'd like to know what kind of tours you're offering because my sources tell me you're pregnant."

The previous numbness overtook Bia again. As she skirted the hedge, looking back at Joey in horror, she almost ran headlong into Aiden.

"Are you pregnant with Hugh Newman's baby?" Joey asked.

The world slowed down into a hazy sort of slow motion as Bia watched Aiden put his hand up and block the creep's camera shot. He put his other arm around Bia to shield her.

"Get that camera out of her face. Let's set the record straight once and for all. There was never anything serious between Bia and Hugh Newman because she's engaged to me."

"Engaged? To you? Since when?"

As Aiden walked Bia back to his place, he put his hand out to block the camera again.

"It's none of your business. Get out of here. Leave us alone."

"Where's the ring?" the guy persisted

"Get out of here." Aiden's voice had an edge.

"Well, at least tell us your name." Obviously, the guy was a veteran at obtaining the news at all costs. Predators like him gave the media a bad name.

"At least kiss your fiancée for us. If you do that, we'll leave you alone."

Aiden stopped and turned to the guy. "Then you'll get that camera out of our faces?"

"Deal," said Joey.

Before she could protest, those lips that she'd contemplated the other day closed over hers. At first, his kiss was surprisingly gentle. He was so tender, tasting like a hint of coffee and something else, something uniquely Aiden. Reflexively, her lips opened under his. As passion overtook her, the gentle kiss morphed into a hard, punishing hunger that consumed her. She wanted the kiss to last forever. She reveled in it, letting it block out all the ugliness of the day. In that moment she wanted this little white lie that Aiden had just told to be true. Right here, right now, she wanted to be Aiden's fiancée. Because Aiden Woods was nothing like Hugh Newman. He was kind and protective and one heck of a good kisser....

Then the kiss ended. Breathlessly, Bia pulled away. The spell was broken. She stood for a moment, her vision slightly blurry, her heart racing, her equilibrium thoroughly thrown. She looked at Aiden, then at Joey, who had finally put down the camera. Then back at Aiden, still feeling the weight of his mouth on hers. All she could do was turn and make a beeline for the sanctuary of Aiden's condo.

Chapter Five

"What the heck did you just do, Aiden?"

When Aiden had first stepped between Bia and the jerk who had been bothering her, her face had been as pale as death. Now, as she collapsed onto the sofa in Aiden's living room, patches of pink stained her cheeks.

As she pressed her fingertips to her mouth, Aiden memorized how her lips had felt, the taste of her, the way she'd kissed him back.

"I got the guy to leave you alone. He stopped asking about Hugh, didn't he?"

"Right, but you also just kissed me in front of the whole world. And you went on record saying we're engaged. What are we supposed to do now? Do we say 'just kidding'!"

She *had* kissed him back, but he knew better than to point that out right now.

"And how did he know that I'm pregnant?" Bia scooted up to the edge of the chair. "Only two people know. You and Maya."

"I sure as hell didn't say anything to anyone. Really, Bia? Do you think I would betray you? What would I stand to gain besides buying myself a whole lot of grief?"

Hell. As soon as the words were out of his mouth, he wished he could take them back. Despite the fact that it was true.

He could tell what she was thinking by the way her eyes flashed: the bachelor party. The night that Duane had been unfaithful. The night that she thought Aiden had led her fiancé astray. It had been a test, and Duane had failed. He didn't deserve a woman like Bia.

She stiffened, sat up straight. "You kind of have a history of that, don't you?"

"Once. You're still blaming me for something that happened once. And, by the way, did I ever mention that I wasn't the one in charge of Duane's actions that night? I thought we agreed to not talk about this again. What I inferred from that agreement was that you accepted that Duane had a will of his own and you had acquitted me. You can't randomly pull this out and use it when you want to skewer me."

She closed her eyes and held up a hand, waving off his words.

A moment later she said, "It's the same guy that was harassing me two months ago, when Hugh was here the first time. Obviously, he has a source who feeds him information."

"So, did this scumbag fly in from L.A.—or wherever the *XYZ* offices are—just to get this film clip?"

"I don't think so. Sometimes the media contracts stringers. They're freelancers who work on an as-needed basis. I'll bet the guy is local. Someone tipped him off the first time Hugh was here a couple months ago, and now he's back at it because of Hugh's accident."

Bia squeezed her eyes shut, the pain evident on her pretty face. It was too bad that this had happened to Hugh. He wasn't exactly an honorable guy, but this... No, not this. Aiden stood and went into the kitchen. He poured two glasses of ice water and brought them back into the living room. He handed one to Bia.

"Thanks," she said. "Putting everything into perspective, I think the news of our *engagement* is going to get lost among the hysteria over Hugh's death. So, I guess it's not the world I'm worried about as much as I'm worried about how we're going to explain this to your mom and our friends and coworkers."

They both sat in silence for a moment.

"I mean, what? Will we *break up* and be one of those couples who remain good friends?"

"Why does everyone's opinion matter, Bia?"

She raked her hands through her hair and continued as if she hadn't heard him. "Just when I think things can't get worse, they do."

"Was kissing me that bad?"

She wouldn't look at him. For a fraction of a second he thought about telling her how he'd wanted to do that a long time ago. How he *should've* done it. Maybe then the situation would be different.

"Why are you doing this, Aiden?" Bia asked.

"I guess I was channeling my inner Prince Valiant," he said, trying to keep the sarcasm out of his voice. She'd kissed him back. He'd felt it as sure as he could feel his heartbeat speed up thinking about the way she'd felt in his arms. The way her lips tasted. "I did it to save you. You're welcome, Princess. Let's just ride this out until the media move on. Okay? There could be worse things."

"Aiden, I don't need to be saved."

"Then why did you call me?"

She was staring at her hands resting in her lap and she gave a quick, one-shoulder shrug.

"I can't have a fake engagement," she said.

"Then I guess we can simply tell everyone the truth, that I did it to save you from the paparazzi."

She rolled her eyes at him. He gritted his teeth and looked away, waiting for his mounting irritation to dissipate. When he looked back, she was staring at him with the most heartrending tenderness he'd ever seen. But it only lasted a moment.

"Do you really think you can fix the engagement you broke up with a fake one?"

"That *I* broke? That's a low blow, B. Do you really want to go there again? I didn't force Duane to cheat on you. If he was any kind of man, he wouldn't have done what he did."

And if he was going to cheat, it would've happened with or without the bachelor party. He didn't say it, but it was hanging in the air, as palpable as if he'd written the words in black marker on the living room wall.

He softened his tone. "Bia, I'm really not a bad guy."

Bia stared out the window a few moments longer before she looked at him. "I know you're not, and I know I have to stop bringing that up. I'm sorry. I appreciate what you did for me out there."

He nodded, feeling as if they'd just made some kind of breakthrough but trying to keep his face neutral. She'd never admitted that before now. It felt like a small victory.

"It's just that...what are we supposed to tell everyone? Your mom, for example? How are we supposed to explain it when we don't get married?"

"Don't worry about that now."

"Of course I'm going to worry about it. Are we going to tell your mom that you're the father of my baby? The one the *XYZ* scumbag asked me about on film? Because if we—or *I*—deny the pregnancy, she and everyone else are going to find out I was lying sooner or later."

She fisted her hands and dug the heels of her palms into her eyes.

"Aiden, this is so messed up. I'm not ready for everyone to know I'm pregnant. I haven't even come to terms with it myself."

"They were going to find out sooner or later," Aiden said.

"Yes, but before this, I was able to deal with it on my terms. Now, it's ready or not."

Aiden moved from the chair to the couch. He took

her hand, and she let him. "We'll figure something out, but for now, don't you think it's better to have someone to lean on through this? At least until the pressure is off?"

She didn't say anything, just looked at him.

"Bia, let me be that person."

Again, she didn't say anything, just stared at him for a long intense moment. Finally, she fell back against the couch and the right corner of her mouth quirked up. "You should know me well enough to know I'd never get engaged without a ring."

"I can take care of that. What kind of a man doesn't give his fiancée a ring?"

He fell back next to her and nudged her with his elbow, a playful gesture to make her smile. She did, even if it was just a half smile, a Mona Lisa smile. He was suddenly aware that their faces were so close that if they each just leaned a little bit he could kiss her again. But she'd have to meet him halfway. He wasn't going to do this by himself.

Right now, it felt as if she wasn't budging. She wasn't even moving her gaze from his. His fingers flexed with the need to reach out and touch her, to trace the line of her jaw from her chin to back to where the bone disappeared behind her ear. He wanted to kiss her there and see if she'd budge then…budge right into his bed.

But, instead, he asked, "Hypothetically, if you were getting engaged, what kind of ring would you want?"

"Hypothetically?"

He nodded.

"I'll show you. Hold on a sec." She pulled her

smartphone out of her pocket and pulled up something on the internet.

"Hypothetically, if I were to get engaged, I'd like this one." She handed him the phone, and he saw a picture of a ring with a deep-set round diamond surrounded by smaller stones. He noticed that there were also thumbnail shots of wedding dresses, flowers, wedding decorations, what looked like ceremony venues.

"What is all this?" he asked. "Is this the wedding you planned with Duane?"

"Absolutely not. It's completely different."

At the risk of rehashing the past, he asked, "So, what happened in the past didn't poison you against marriage?"

"No, if it didn't poison me against *you,* why should it poison me against marriage? I mean, it certainly made me not want to marry Duane, but I'd love to get married someday. I want a family—and I'm obviously getting that sooner than I thought."

The faraway look in her eyes changed to one of sorrow. She clasped her hands over her stomach. "But I guess this might be a game changer."

"Not with the right guy." He continued scrolling through her wedding photo gallery. "So, women do this in their spare time? They plan weddings?"

"For the record, a girl can dream."

"For the record, I get that. I guess. The princess is a hopeless romantic. I've never seen this side of you before."

Their gazes locked again, and the way she was looking at him almost made him want to bridge the distance—cover the ground for both of them—and kiss her again. If she hadn't looked away, he would've done it.

But the sea change reminded him that being fast and reckless with Bia wasn't the way to go. The chemistry was there. It always had been, but now it was starting to age into something viable.

Patience, Grasshopper. Patience.

"I think I have a pretty good idea who is leaking this personal information to the paparazzi," she said. "I'm going to find out today."

Later that afternoon, Bia pulled into the Maya's Chocolates parking lot. She hadn't even called ahead to say she was coming because she wanted to look Maya in the eyes when she asked her the question. If Aiden wasn't the one who had leaked the news about the pregnancy, it had to be Maya or Nurse Flirty. Somehow her gut was telling her that despite Flirty's wandering eye, she didn't seem the type who would break laws and betray a patient's confidentiality.

But God, who could you trust these days? Someone had alerted the media. Bia would be able to tell by Maya's reaction if she was the guilty one.

Bia was relieved that Maya's car, a bright yellow Volkswagen Beetle, was in the lot. She steered her navy blue Volvo into the parking space next to Maya's car. The parking lot ran alongside the bungalow. It probably used to be a side yard years ago, when the place was a single-family home. A couple of men were working at the far end of the small parking lot. It looked as if they were doing some carpentry work. Probably something last-minute for the grand opening.

Bia sat in her car for a moment, replaying in her head the last conversation she'd had with Maya, trying to remember if she'd said anything that should've been a tip-off that she was going to talk to the media. Bia couldn't recall anything. In fact, Maya had been warm and sympathetic. She'd been a friend. It was strange this so-called friendship she'd formed with this woman who'd seemingly come out of nowhere to open a business in the middle of nowhere. What was even more peculiar was that each time Bia had doubted Maya, something had reeled her back in. Which was why she was there right now. Rather than just writing her off and avoiding her.

No, she had to see Maya's eyes when she asked her the question.

Maya was all smiles when she answered the door and let Bia in.

"*Bonjour!* What a wonderful surprise." Maya leaned in and planted a kiss on Bia's cheek. "And your timing is perfect. I just got back from lunch and running some errands. Come in. Have you had your calcium today? Shall I make us some drinking chocolate?"

Oh. At first glance things seemed to be okay. Normal. Maybe she was good at bluffing? If she was, then it meant things like right and wrong didn't matter to her. But it wasn't fair to judge Maya guilty until she asked her straight-out.

Maya was already walking ahead of Bia, gesturing her to follow her to the kitchen. Bia did.

Right away, Maya busied herself gathering the items for the hot chocolate. "Did you need some more information for the article?"

"No, actually, I came to ask you a personal question."

Maya stopped pouring milk into the copper pot, set down the milk carton and turned her full attention to Bia.

"Sure," she said, her eyes sparkling, actually looking a little hopeful. "Ask me anything."

Rarely at a loss for words, Bia was unsure how to start. So she decided to begin gently, from the beginning.

"Did you hear the news about Hugh?"

The smile faded from Maya's face. "I'm sorry to say I did. It's such a tragedy. I didn't want to say anything in case you didn't know."

"Yes, it is a tragedy," Bia said, keeping her gaze trained on Maya's face. "I was at work when I heard the news. I was pretty shocked."

"I can imagine. Did you ever get a chance to talk to him?"

"No, I didn't get to talk to him personally. But when I heard, I decided to walk over to a friend's place that is only a couple of blocks away from my office. On the way, the same guy who accosted me the last time Hugh was in town was waiting for me outside. He and his driver followed me to my friend Aiden's."

"Oh, I'm so sorry," Maya said. "The last thing you needed at a time like that was someone—how do you say it?—barging in on you in your time of sorrow." Her face bore the look of genuine sadness. Not the oops-I-did-a-bad-thing kind of sadness, but more of a genuine, from the heart, sorry-for-a-friend's-troubles expression.

"I know. It was pretty awful. He was pointing a camcorder at me while he was quizzing me about how I felt after learning about Hugh's accident."

"For shame." Maya sounded truly incensed.

"That's not the worst part." Bia paused to see if she could pick up on any perceptible change in Maya's demeanor. But the woman held steady.

"What?" she asked. "What happened?"

"Somehow the guy knew I was pregnant."

Maya gasped. "How? How did he know?"

"I...don't know. The only two people I told were you and Aiden. I know Aiden didn't tip him off. In fact, he almost punched the guy when he wouldn't leave me alone. It will probably be on the next episode of *XYZ*."

"What is this *XYZ* that you speak of?"

"It's a tabloid television show. You've never heard of it?"

"No, I haven't. It is not my kind of television program, you see."

Again, Bia watched Maya closely. She simply frowned and resumed making the hot chocolate, but she didn't act nervous or defensive.

"So, you didn't see the show the first time the guy was harassing me? Back when Hugh was in town for the Doctor's Ball?"

Maya shook her head and stirred, holding the copper pot by its handle. "I read about the accounts of you and the actor, but I didn't see it on television."

"Well, you didn't miss anything important. The footage they shot today will probably air tomorrow night. I'm DVRing it because I don't know if I can bring myself to watch. But what I want to talk to you about is who could've tipped off this guy? How did he know I'm pregnant?"

Maya frowned and tilted her head to one side, as if she was thinking, genuinely trying to solve the puzzle. "This Aiden you speak of, you are one hundred percent sure he is trustworthy?"

"I would trust him with my life." Bia couldn't blunt the edge in her tone.

Maya's face softened. "You would? He is that good to you?"

Bia nodded.

"I would like to meet this Aiden who means so much to you."

"Why?" Startled by this suggestion, Bia mentally backpedaled a little bit. Was this Maya's way to distract her, to throw her off course? A sleight of hand to get her talking about Aiden or anything else to divert her attention?

"Why? I am just interested in this man who has captured your heart."

"What? Wait. No! You have this all wrong. The relationship I have with Aiden isn't like that, and that's not what I came here to talk to you about. Maya, if you and Aiden are the only two who know about my pregnancy, and I know for a fact that Aiden didn't tell anyone… Well, you do the math."

Maya regarded Bia for a moment. Her expression was inscrutable. Then she turned and took two demitasse cups down from a cupboard and poured the chocolate.

"I can see how this might look to you, but I can assure you that I am not the one who alerted the press."

"If not you, then who? I mean, how can I believe you didn't?"

Maya carried the two cups on saucers and set them on the table. "Please have a seat, Bia. There is something I must tell you. I didn't want it to come out like this, but, given the circumstances, you must know now."

What? Was Maya going to confess?

Had she needed the money to finance her new location—not that two stories about an actor's affair with an ordinary no-name would bring in the big bucks.

Bia remained standing. "Look, we don't have to drag this out. If you tipped him off, just tell me. Fast and simple. I need to know."

"Sit down, Bia." Maya's voice was calm. "This is not about the tabloid reporter. This is an entirely different matter."

Something in Maya's voice had Bia lowering herself onto the chair. If it wasn't about *XYZ*…she was almost afraid to know.

"About a year and a half ago, your father contacted me."

Bia did a double take. "My *father?* How did you and my father know each other?"

Maya looked away as she picked up her chocolate and sipped it. "Actually, we never met. Not in person. But when he was diagnosed with cancer, he contacted me to tell me. You see, he knew he was terminal and it was very important to your father that you not be alone in the world after he passed on."

Suddenly, Bia felt as if she'd slipped and had fallen down a rabbit hole. She could see where this story might be headed, but she couldn't let herself land there until Maya said the words.

"So…my dying father contacted you, this person he'd never met, and asked you to look out for my well-being? I'm a grown woman. I've been living on my own for years. Why would he do that?"

"Because, Bia, I am your birth mother."

Now Bia was free-falling down the rabbit hole. She had never felt so out of control of her life. And it just kept getting worse. When was it going to stop? When was life going to quit punching her in the stomach long enough so that she could catch her breath and grasp all the changes that were happening? It was as if the universe had taken her life, turned it upside down and was continuing to shake her until everything that had ever made sense fell away from her world.

"I know this is a shock, but please say something," Maya said.

What? What am I supposed to say? Why did you give me up? Why are you back now? Are we supposed to pick up and act as if we've always had a relationship?

"My father contacted you?"

"Yes. He told me of his condition but asked me not to contact you until after he was gone."

"If he wanted…this—" Bia gestured back and forth between them "—why wouldn't he introduce us? Why wouldn't he have been part of our reunion? I don't understand."

Maya's expression was as gentle as a Madonna's. "Probably for the same reason he couldn't tell you himself that you were adopted. He told me about the letter he was leaving for you for after he'd passed. He'd arranged for his attorney to notify me once he'd passed on. I didn't want to tell you this way, Bia. I wanted you to get to know me better before I told you. Especially given your pregnancy and Hugh's death. It's a lot to digest."

"I just don't understand why he had to do it that way," Bia said. "Finding out that I'm adopted didn't change the way I feel for him, but I was disappointed that he couldn't tell me himself."

"I wish I had the answers for you, but I hope this helps you believe that I would never betray your confidence. Especially not to the media."

Bia had so many questions. Why did Maya give her up in the first place? What was she expecting now? But another more pressing question remained. "Then who did?"

"Perhaps I can help you get to the bottom of it?"

"How would you do that?"

"I don't know, but I can think about it. I want to be a part of your life, Bia. I want to catch up on all I missed out on with you and to know my grandchild. Will you let me?"

It was too much, too fast, too soon.

"I need time to think, time to process everything." Bia stood. "Please excuse me. I need to go now."

Chapter Six

"How is it that you always seem to know when I need you?" Bia asked.

Aiden stood in the threshold of Bia's house. She looked sexy in those jeans that hugged her in all the right places. He had an almost uncontrollable urge to lean in, draw those curves against him and kiss her. He reminded himself that even though he had made up his mind that she would be his, she wasn't quite ready yet. If he rushed things, he might blow it. It was best to take things slowly.

That's why he'd hesitated today when he'd found himself at the jewelry store looking at diamond rings. He'd walked away and come back three different times before he'd convinced himself that buying a ring was the right thing to do.

If he was going to make this happen, he needed to do it right. So he'd purchased the ring.

"Guess I'm just talented that way. So, you need me, huh? Was the jackass back?"

Bia shook her head. "Something different. Just when I think that all the crazy things in the world that can happen have laid themselves at my feet, *bam!*" She clapped her hands together. "Something else jumps out at me—like a scary clown in a jack-in-the-box."

She stepped aside and motioned for him to come in.

"I met my birth mother."

Aiden stopped and turned around. "What?"

"Yes. Well, actually, I've known her for a couple of months now. Only I had no idea until today. She wanted to wait until—" Bia made air quotes with her fingers "—*the right time* to tell me."

"And she decided now is the right time?"

Bia nodded.

"Who is she?"

Bia closed her eyes and took a long, slow deep breath. The tension was evident on her face. Aiden wanted to pull her into his arms and assure her that everything would be okay. He'd make sure of it. Come hell or high water.

"It's Maya." Bia's usually strong, confident voice was a whisper.

"Chocolate-maker Maya?"

Bia nodded, looking so fragile, as if she might break at any moment.

"You saw her today, and she thought now was the *right time?*"

Bia told Aiden about what had transpired with

Maya after she'd left him. "She hadn't planned on telling me today. But I went to see her and asked her if she was the press informant. That's when she told me. She promised she would never betray me. Now that I've had a little bit of time to step back and think about it, I get it. Sort of. But I told her I need some time to process everything. In the meantime, that brings up an entirely new conundrum. If neither you nor she told the *XYZ* guy, who did? The only other people who know are Dr. Porter and your nurse girlfriend and the others in the office—they could've been talking among themselves."

Aiden grimaced. "She's not my girlfriend. Especially not if she spills secrets like that. You know, it's against the law to leak medical information."

"I know." Bia smirked. "At first, I couldn't put it together. It didn't make sense. I'd never met anyone in Dr. Porter's office. I figured it had to be the same person who tipped off the tabloid a couple of months ago. So, the likelihood of someone in that office being the *XYZ* connection seemed like a stretch." She held up her index finger. "But then, I went to the *XYZ* website and found out there is a 'hot tip' number. They offer a reward for stories that end up on the air. Anyone can call in the scoop. So, the person who tipped them off about my doctor's appointment didn't necessarily have to be the original informant. Really, once a story like that is out, people are looking for the least little anything to call in a tip. Especially if there's a chance of a financial reward."

"If you really believe you can trust Maya, it almost

has to be someone in Porter's office. Seems like they're the only suspects, doesn't it? How do we prove it?"

"I have no idea. I thought about calling Dr. Porter and telling him what's happened, suggesting that he have a talk with his staff, just in case, but then I thought better of it. I decided I don't want to go there. It's too big of an accusation without proof positive. Plus, it would only draw more attention to the situation. I'm just going to leave it alone, switch doctors and keep my head down."

They looked at each other for a silent moment.

"Have you thought about what we are going to say when people ask when we're getting married?" Aiden asked. "We should probably talk about this so we have our stories straight."

"All we have to tell them is we haven't set a date yet."

"So, you're saying you want to move forward with Plan Engagement?" Aiden asked.

Bia's throat worked, and then she raised her chin and gave a single resolute nod. "I think so. I mean, I don't see any other way around it. Since it's likely that the reporter is still on high alert."

"Then I need to ask a favor," Aiden said.

"Sure," Bia said. "Anything. God knows you're making a huge sacrifice for me by going through with this charade. I can't imagine what this is going to do to your love life."

His gaze fell to her lips and then found her eyes again. *You have no idea. Not yet, anyway.*

"Before the show airs tonight," Aiden said. "I want to tell my mother. I don't want her to hear it on television. And what about Maya? Did you say anything to her?"

Bia shook her head.

"You don't want to tell her before she hears about it through the mass media?"

"Aiden, I don't know what I want to do about her yet. I need time to think. I mean, you haven't even met her yet. She knows about you, but—"

"You told her about me?"

"I told her you were my best friend."

There was something in her expression, something in her eyes, that made him believe *best friend* was a good thing. It wasn't *friend zone* best friend. It was best friend with a whole lot more potential.

"You do need to tell your mom." Bia sighed audibly. "I just can't quite make peace with telling her we're engaged when we really aren't. I know I said I wanted to go through with it, but I've met your mother. I just have a bad feeling that she's going to see right through this scheme. I wish there was some way around that."

"That really bothers you, doesn't it?"

"Well, yes. It should bother you, too. Unless you make a habit of lying to your mother?"

"That's a low blow," he said. "You know I don't."

"I know," she said. "I'm sorry. It's just…one more thing that feels as if it's spinning out of control."

"Okay. I know how to fix this," he said.

"Do tell."

He walked across the room and pulled Bia to her feet.

"What are you doing?" she protested.

He dropped down on one knee and took her hands in his. "Bia Anderson, will you marry me?"

"Aiden, stop it."

He knew her so well that he'd anticipated that she would balk at the suggestion…at first. "Bia, I am proposing to you. If you don't want to lie to my mother, I would suggest that you accept my proposal. It's as simple as that. Say, 'Yes, Aiden, I'll marry you,' and then we will be engaged. There you go. No lying to anyone."

"But we're lying to ourselves."

"Only if you believe that's what we're doing."

"What? Are you saying this is real?"

He didn't answer her.

"What about the tiny little detail of the wedding that will never happen?" she asked.

"We will just have to cross that bridge when we come to it. Come on, B. Live for the moment."

She frowned. "I know that's your philosophy, Aiden, but I have to start thinking about the future."

"The immediate future is that reporter who is still lurking out there. Do you want to deal with him? Do you want me to explain to him that I was just protecting you when I said we were engaged? Because he's not going to go away unless he thinks he doesn't have a story. If word gets around that we told him we're engaged and we're not, then he's going to be on you like white on rice, until he proves that his initial hunch was right. So, I'll ask you one more time. Bia, will you marry me?"

She opened her mouth to say something, but no

sound came out. She clamped her lips shut, a per-plexed look on her face.

"It's a simple yes or no question, Princess," Aiden said. His knee was starting to ache, the remnants of an old college football injury. "This offer is only on the table as long as my knee can stand this cruel and un-usual punishment. So what's it going to be, yes or no?"

She blinked at him, looking a little stunned.

"Aiden, if we do this, we have to do it right."

"Isn't that what we're doing?"

"Well, yes. Sort of. But what I mean is if we do this…this…" She gestured between them with her hand. "You have to play the part."

"Right. And that means?"

"I mean, you can't be engaged to me and be seen around town with a bunch of different women. Even if this isn't *real,* I don't want a replay of what hap-pened with Duane. Everybody was talking about it, and I looked like a fool. I don't want to go through that again."

"I understand. I promise you're the only woman I will be seen with, Bia. Now, for the sake of my knee, can we please get on with this?"

She nodded. "But wait. We need a ring."

"If we had a ring, would you say yes?" he asked.

"I don't want you to go out and buy one. Wait, hold on a second. I have an idea." She left the room and re-turned a moment later with a small white box.

"This is a birthstone ring that my mother—er…my adopted mother wore." Bia opened the box and showed Aiden the thin gold band with a small purple stone.

"My father gave it to me a long time ago, but it's a

little bit too big. I never wore it because I was afraid it would slip off my finger. I didn't want to lose it."

Bia gazed at the ring. "After she died, there wasn't another woman in the world for my father. That's why he never remarried."

Aiden knew the feeling. There was only one woman in the world for him. No matter how he'd tried to get over her, his heart had always belonged to Bia. Always had, always would.

"It's not a diamond engagement ring," he said.

"That's okay."

She could be so stubborn sometimes. He was surprised that she wasn't holding out for exactly what she wanted. It took a little fun out of his plan. He took the ring box from her, took it out of the box and studied it.

"This is nice," he said. "It has a lot of sentimental value. But the way I see it, there's two problems. First one is it doesn't fit you. It might slip off your finger. It would be a real shame for you to lose it since it means so much to you. The second problem is that it's not an engagement ring. Any fiancée of mine would wear a diamond ring."

He pulled the small black box out of his jacket pocket and opened it. "I was thinking something like this might be more appropriate."

Bia gaped at him with large green eyes. "Aiden, what did you do?"

"It looks pretty good, doesn't it?" he asked.

"Please tell me this isn't a real diamond. Because I know you wouldn't go out and buy a diamond ring for this."

"I would if I had extra cash lying around begging

to be spent," he said. "It's as real as we want it to be. Like I said, my fiancée will wear a ring we can both be proud of."

"You would really do this for me?" she asked. "Swear off other women for a while and pretend to be engaged to me?"

He smiled. "Apparently so."

Bia was finally silent, fresh out of conditions, even if she did look a little overwhelmed. Aiden got back down on one knee and took her hand in his.

"Bia Anderson, will you do me the honor of being my wife?"

She stared at him for a moment. A vague light seemed to pass between them, and then the air in the room shifted.

"Yes, Aiden, I will."

As he slid the ring on her finger, he silently vowed to hold her to that promise.

Sunday evening, Bia sat in her living room alone with a cup of herbal tea, prepared to watch the fateful edition of *XYZ Celebrity News.*

Aiden had wanted to come over and watch it with her, but Bia had told him she had to do this alone. With all the other hoopla surrounding the *XYZ* reporter ambush, Aiden's fake but all-too-real-feeling proposal and the discovery that Maya was her birth mother, she hadn't even had time to properly mourn Hugh.

It was the strangest feeling. She wasn't in love with Hugh. In fact, she really hadn't even liked the guy during his last few days on earth, after he'd shirked his responsibilities to her and the baby. But the facts remained that he was the father of her child and he was much too young to die. It felt odd—sad and odd—to contemplate that he was no longer in this world.

As she lifted her cup to her lips, the light caught the diamond on her finger, making it wink and glint. After she took a sip, she returned the cup to its saucer and held up her hand.

It hadn't escaped her that just before Aiden had slipped the ring on her finger, he had changed the wording of his proposal and asked her to be his wife.

It had felt real. The earnest look on his face and the intense way he'd looked her in the eyes had caused her breath to hitch and made her stomach do an odd somersault. If she didn't watch it, she could let herself get caught up in the fantasy. Not only was Aiden a devastatingly handsome guy; he made her feel safe and cared for…and the side of her that had let its guard down had felt electric as he'd slipped the ring on her finger. She reminded herself that she had to make sure she kept both feet firmly planted in reality. She couldn't forget herself.

While Aiden was a great friend, falling for someone like him was a recipe for heartache. God knew—between Duane and Hugh—she'd had enough of that for a lifetime.

She put her hand on her stomach. She was going to be a mother. That was a total game changer. Now she no longer had the luxury of taking stupid chances. Now every decision she made had to have her child at its heart. Since the mishap with Duane's bachelor party, Aiden had taken great pains to prove himself a top-notch friend. No matter how handsome, sexy and downright tempting she found him, she couldn't afford to take a chance that risky. Because there were fewer things riskier than trying to get Aiden to commit to a long-term relationship.

The red and black of the *XYZ Celebrity News* logo caught her attention as it flashed across the screen. The show was starting. Her stomach knotted as she picked up the remote and unmuted the TV.

Here we go.

Hugh's accident was the lead story. The verbal subheadline: "Was Hugh Newman out *celebrating* the news that he was going to be a father before his fatal crash?"

Seeing his photo emblazoned with his birthdate and death date made it real. Her eyes filled with tears. As crazy as it sounded, somewhere deep in Bia's subconscious she'd hoped that this would somehow turn out to be an urban legend that had gotten out of control. One huge publicity stunt. She had no idea why seeing it on this skanky tabloid show made it feel official to her and real—other than the fact that these skeevy reporters were the ones who had drilled to the heart of what was real when they'd reported her affair with Hugh the first time. Sure, they were easily diverted by Hugh's camp and a total curtailing of contact between the two of them, but they'd gotten it right.

The camera captured the grim-faced *XYZ* ringleader as he sat leaning back in his chair, with his legs propped up on his desk, managing to restrain himself from cracking jokes as he and his minions dished about the few details they'd managed to uncover about Hugh's accident.

Blahblahblahblah car crash. *Blahblahblahblah* returning from party. *Blahblahblahblah* waiting for toxicology reports. *Blahblahblahblah* alone in the car.

Next, they broke to a shot of Kristin Capistrano sobbing hysterically. Bia's heart went out to the woman. If love could be weighed in tears, Kristin had been in deep.

Then, there it was—the somewhat blurry photo that had made the rounds two months before: Bia in that blue sundress. She made a mental note to donate it. If it wasn't such a nice dress, she'd burn it. She and Hugh were sitting at a patio table at Bistro Saint-Germain in downtown Celebration. They did look rather cozy the way they were leaning into one another. Bia was smiling, and Hugh looked as if he was playing with a wisp of her hair. As an *XYZ* minion rehashed the history of Bia and Hugh, his fellow minions made snide comments about the nature of the *tours* she allegedly gave. Of course, they couldn't remain somber and dignified for long. Someone had to go there, had to say it, "Well, at least we know she's not an *escort* in the old-fashioned sense of the word. We've learned that Hugh Newman's—" he cleared his throat "—*tour guide* is actually a pretty smart cookie. She is the editor of Celebration's local newspaper. I don't know when she finds time to offer private tours."

Yuck. Yuck. Yuck. Did they have no respect? No dignity?

And then the coup de grâce: Bia flinched as her own image appeared on the screen. She felt sick as she relived the way the *XYZ* minion harassed her, dogging her every move. And then there was Aiden. He swooped in, put one arm around her and stretched out the other, momentarily blocking the camera's view with the palm of his. Then he stepped back and claimed she was his fiancée.

Her stomach gave an unexpected little flutter at Aiden's protectiveness.

"Get that camera out of her face. Let's set the record straight once and for all. There was never anything serious between Bia and Hugh Newman because she's engaged to me."

"Engaged? To you? Since when?"

The flutter intensified as she watched the kiss they'd shared replay in living color on the television set. She could feel the weight of his lips on hers—just a little chapped and extremely skilled…what with all the practice he'd had.

It was like an out-of-body experience watching herself kissing this man who had become her best friend. A friend with whom she'd struggled through a love-hate relationship to get to the point where they were now.

Why is it feeling an awful lot like love now?

She shook away the preposterous thought.

This was *Aiden*. He certainly had never been Prince Charming. Prince Charming probably wasn't such a darn good kisser.

In the background now, they were saying something about how Hugh and Kristin had been scheduled to film a movie in Celebration, "a quaint, picturesque town that harkens back to simpler days."

Ahh, simpler days. The days before she'd met Hugh

and started having inappropriate thoughts about her best friend.

"However, with the recent turn of events, the future of the film is uncertain. For now, inside sources say the film is shelved. At least until they can figure out who will take over the role that Newman had been cast to play."

So many things were uncertain.

Life itself was fragile and tentative. You could spend your whole life protecting your heart so that it never got trampled on again, so that someone like Duane or Hugh didn't misuse it or hurt you. You could spend your entire life being careful and then die alone unbroken and unfulfilled.

She glanced down at her left hand. The diamond winked at her. Maybe it was time to explore the possibilities and live a little.

Chapter Seven

"Congratulations, Bia," said Nicole. "I can't believe you didn't tell us you were engaged. We had to find out on national television? You're so unromantic."

Nicole smiled, but underneath those perfect white teeth Bia was sure there were fangs ready to come out and bite her.

"You know me," Bia said as she made herself a cup of decaffeinated tea in the newspaper office's break room. "I'm generally a private person. If it makes you feel any better, Aiden and I hadn't really planned on announcing our engagement on national television. It was just one of those things."

"But are you…?" Nicole patted her belly.

"Am I what?"

Thank you, XYZ. The questions of the day had

been about the engagement and the pregnancy. The ultra-brazen had even gone as far as to ask who the father was—Hugh or Aiden.

Bia had leveled the ones who had had the audacity to ask with a stare that had made them wish they'd kept their mouths shut.

"I mean, there's private and then there's *private*," Nicole said. "No one even knew you and Aiden were dating. Or that you were—"

Bia pierced her with a look that stopped her mid-sentence. Then she took a quart of half-and-half out of the refrigerator and stirred some into her tea. "As I said, Nicole, I'm a very private person. I don't like to discuss my personal life at work. And speaking of. Both of us need to get back to it."

She turned and walked to her desk. All the while, she could feel Nicole's gaze burning holes into her back. Bia had to admit, the woman's tenacity was one of the things that made her a good reporter. She seemed to have a sharp bull detector and she wouldn't let an issue drop when she had a hunch she was right. Ha. Maybe Nicole should get a job with *XYZ*.

As Bia sat down at her desk, she felt bad for thinking that about her employee. When the scrutiny wasn't turned on her, Bia admired Nicole's tenacity. But when she wouldn't take no for an answer (which was usually when she didn't get what she wanted) or the tables were turned, Bia wanted to ship the woman off to parts unknown.

Well, Nicole could ask all the questions she wanted. Bia wasn't required to answer.

She clicked on the email icon on her computer and

checked the damage that had accrued in the time that it took her to get her tea.

Twenty-six new emails. Before she even opened them, she could tell that five of them were from other news outlets requesting interviews.

Thanks to *XYZ* announcing to the world where she worked, she'd been inundated by the curious and the newshounds alike.

For heaven's sake. What part of engaged to another man did they not understand? She highlighted each of the emails and clicked the spam button. "There. That's better."

She was screening all her calls today, as well. She'd set the phone to automatically and silently deposit all calls into her voice mailbox. Otherwise, how was she supposed to get any work done? That's why the sound of her desk phone ringing startled her out of her concentration.

It was Candice, the receptionist. "Hi, Bia, I just wanted to let you know that Mr. Montgomery just arrived and he is on his way back to see you."

Drew Montgomery. Her boss. *Wonderful*...though she should have seen a visit from him coming from a mile away. Strange that he hadn't tried to call her first.

"Thank you, Candice."

Bia stood and met Drew at her office door.

"Hi, Drew, good to see you. Come in, please." She put on her most professional smile, determined to prove that nothing had changed in the newsroom. Despite how she had found herself in the news lately, everything was under control at the *Dallas Journal of Business and Development*.

Drew stepped into her office and took a seat in one of the chairs across from her desk. She shut the door. Once she'd reclaimed her seat, Drew said, "So, I understand congratulations are in order."

Reflexively, Bia's thumb went to the back of her engagement ring. She glanced down at the diamond. It was still a bit startling every time she saw it on her finger.

"Thank you," she said, deciding to let Drew take the lead in the conversation.

"I see your *XYZ* buddy was back," he said. "Do you need any help with that?"

Bia squinted at him, unsure what he meant. "I'm pretty confident the most recent ambush was the last, given the sad turn of events with Hugh Newman."

"Yeah, that was pretty shocking," Drew said. "And sad."

Bia nodded.

"I don't foresee any reasons for *XYZ* to need to interview me in the future. Now that Aiden and I are engaged, I'm no longer newsworthy."

"Yeah, about that," said Drew. "I've known for a long time that the guy is crazy about you, but I had no idea the two of you were serious."

His comment made Bia's heart race, and then she wanted to squirm. It wasn't like that between her and Aiden. That's why their relationship worked. That's why they were so good together. That's why they were such good—

She couldn't bring herself to say the word *friends* anymore, and that just about gave her a panic attack.

Now that her dad was gone, Aiden was all that she

had. If she lost him because of this… Behind the desk her hand found her belly, and she thought of Maya.

Actually, she wasn't alone anymore. At least she didn't have to be.

A baby and her own birth mother, who seemed to be on such an even keel, so patient and kind. Even if she had been a surprise in Bia's life, Maya had the personal endorsement of her boss's wife. And Caroline's friends.

So much had changed, and it seemed as if more changes were happening on a daily basis. Maybe she needed to take a step back and give Maya a chance.

"Anything else you'd like to share?" Drew asked.

Bia knew that he was hinting about the pregnancy. He was a decent guy and wouldn't come right out and ask until she was ready to bring it up.

She glanced out the window that overlooked the newsroom. Everyone seemed to be busy—on the phone or pounding away at their computers. She might as well confide in Drew. He'd know about the baby sooner or later.

"Well, actually, yes, there is. I'm going to have a baby in about seven months."

"Congratulations to you and Aiden," he said.

She didn't correct him. She glanced at the ring that Aiden had put on her finger. Aiden was the one who had the most to lose—taking himself off the dating market, pretending to be the father of another man's child and being willing to make everyone think that he wanted to marry her. She needed to be grateful enough to graciously accept this ultimate gift of friendship he was offering her.

"Thank you, Drew. I promise nothing will change here. I plan to work up to my due date and then take minimal time off. So, I can assure you there's nothing to worry about."

Drew nodded. "I was never worried. I can step in and help pick up the slack while you're out, and I know Nicole is eager to prove herself around here."

I'm sure she is. "She's a real go-getter, isn't she? But we have a long time between now and my due date. So let's not worry about that now."

"The real reason I'm here is because Caroline wanted me to invite Aiden and you to dinner next week. Are you free?"

"Thank you. I'm sure we can make time. Let me talk to Aiden. I'll let you know."

Bia felt the weight of somebody's gaze on her. She glanced out the window into the newsroom, and saw Nicole, unsmiling and watching Drew and her. Bia held Nicole's gaze until the woman looked away.

Yeah, *she's a real go-getter.* For some reason, Bia didn't trust her. Usually, she admired ambitious women. However, Nicole elevated ambition to aggressive. It was a shame she had to be that way. Bia knew she needed to honor her gut feeling and watch her back.

Chapter Eight

Today was the day. Opening day for Maya's Chocolates.

Maya's stomach was all aflutter. She'd put a lot of time, effort and money into this venture. She hoped today would go smoothly.

Aw, who was she kidding? She didn't simply want it to go smoothly; she wanted it to be a smashing success. She had hired three full-time sales clerks. She'd spent the past two days training them and felt good about the team she'd created.

She glanced around the shop. Everything was in place. The chocolate had been delivered yesterday, and she had spent the entire day up to her elbows in cocoa making several batches of handmade confections for the special day. Being in the kitchen was also good therapy to keep her mind off the fact that she hadn't heard from Bia since she'd broken the news that she was her birth mother. Maya was determined to give Bia her space until she had the opportunity to come to terms with the news. She knew it was a lot to handle on top of everything else she had gone through recently. Maya simply wished that Bia could see that now of all times it would be good to have a family member—a mother—to help her through.

So Maya had decided to give her time to think about it, or she'd wait at least until after the shop's grand opening. If she hadn't heard from her by then, she might start thinking of another approach. She couldn't allow herself to think that Bia might completely shun her. Of course, it was a possibility, but she just wasn't going to go there.

Especially not today.

Maya glanced at her watch. It had belonged to her grandmother. So it seemed particularly appropriate to wear it today. It was as if her grandmother and her mother were there with her. The only person missing was Bia, but Maya had seen the article that had appeared in the *Dallas Journal of Business and Development* just as Bia had promised.

Maya told herself that was second best to Bia being there in person.

It was nine-thirty. The shop would open in half an hour. Maya straightened her scarf, fluffed her hair and said a silent prayer for a great first day.

She walked from the kitchen onto the shop floor. Her three sales clerks, Susan, Paulina and Meg, were chatting away excitedly. They immediately quieted and jumped to attention when Maya walked into the room. They were dressed all in black as Maya had instructed them. Paulina had a feather duster in her hand and was swishing and swiping it over the fixtures. Maya hoped the girl would be as conscientious after the newness had worn off the adventure and the dust had had a chance to settle.

"Good morning, my chickens," Maya said. "You three look lovely. Thank you for dressing appropriately and for being here on time. This is the beginning of a wonderful adventure for all of us, and I'm glad you are here with me. We will open our doors at precisely ten o'clock. I hope we will have so much business that it will prove impossible for us to take a break. However, I will make sure that you get some time to refresh. I have posted the schedule in the kitchen on the bulletin board above the table."

Maya was just getting ready to go over the procedure for utilizing the cash drawer when a knock sounded at the door. She turned around to see Bia standing there with an armful of flowers. Her heart nearly leaped out of her chest.

"Please excuse me," Maya said. "We have a very special visitor."

Maya worried the hem of her scarf as she made her way to the door to let Bia in.

She had come.

Bia was her *first-footer*. It had to be a fabulous sign. While the Scottish tradition of first-footing said that the first person to cross a home's threshold after midnight on New Year's Eve would determine the family's luck for the year, Maya thought it auspicious that Bia was the first person to cross her threshold on the first day of her new business. The employees had used the employee entrance in the back.

Maya opened the door and greeted Bia enthusiastically.

"I am so happy to see you," she said. "I can't even begin to tell you."

"These are for you," said Bia. She handed Maya the flowers.

"Thank you so very much," Maya said, bringing the mix of white flowers to her nose. The flowers, which were in a tall glass vase, contained freesia, carnations and lilies that were tied with a silver ribbon. "These will look lovely on the wrap stand. I can't believe I neglected to get fresh flowers."

"Do you see these?" Bia asked. She indicated green stalklike limbs sticking out in the middle of the flowers. Maya had thought it was greenery.

"It's lucky bamboo," said Bia. "There are nine stalks and they represent good fortune. Even after the flowers fade, the bamboo will thrive. It lasts for years. If not forever."

Maya was so touched that tears came to her eyes. She smiled at Bia. "Thank you so much for this." Her words caught in her throat, and she took a moment to gather her composure. "It means so much that you're here this morning."

"I couldn't let you open without sending good wishes and good fortune," Bia said as Maya set the vase of flowers next to the register. "Did you see the article in today's paper?"

"I did. It was wonderful. Thank you so very much. For that and for being here now."

"Drew tells me you're invited to the dinner party they're throwing. Are you going?"

"I wouldn't miss it."

"I'm glad," said Bia. "It will be good to spend some time with you. But you must be swamped getting ready to open the doors. Look, people are lining up already. I won't keep you."

Bia gestured toward the door, where a small crowd had gathered.

"You see—you're already bringing me good luck," Maya said. "Before you arrived, nobody was out there. Now look at them."

Bia hitched her purse up onto her shoulder. "Maybe once you get the business up and running, we can meet for lunch or coffee or something?"

Maya put a hand on Bia's arm. "I would love that. And, of course, there's always dinner next week."

Within an hour of the shop being open, the store was overrun with people. Maya and the staff had to keep going into the storeroom off the kitchen to bring out more chocolate to restock the shelves. It looked as if that lucky bamboo was working, after all. Or maybe it was the good fortune of her first-footer. More likely it was the attention that Bia had garnered through the article that had run that morning. Either way, Maya was grateful for the blessing of her daughter.

She rang up a box of truffles, a candy gift basket and a collection of chocolate bars for a woman who said she was buying the candy for her grandchildren. "That will be $106.42, please." As the woman fished in her wallet for two pennies, Maya thought she saw someone familiar out of the corner of her eye. A man. It was his posture. The sight nearly made her heart stop.

Ian?

It couldn't be. Maya knew that, although her heart didn't seem to understand. A knot of people blocked her view and she craned her neck to see around them. No luck, though.

Her heart sank.

How many times had she thought she'd seen Ian's face in the crowd before? Too many times to count. Ian was dead. He wasn't coming back. She knew that. It was probably just her imagination conjuring up his image on this special day.

If wishes were chocolate…

Hmm…

She'd have to remember that, maybe use it in an advertisement.

She forced her cheeriest smile as she thanked the woman for her purchase.

"How often will you have handmade chocolate?" the woman asked.

"Of course, it will depend on the demand, but I think I will try to make fresh batches twice a week." Maya gestured toward a silver guest book. "Would you care to sign up for our mailing list? That way I can let you know when the fresh batches of chocolate are available. I'll also be able to tell you about specials and events that we're having."

Maya thought about getting a neon sign to put in the window. One she could light up when the handmade chocolate was available. She filed that idea away with the ad idea.

"Absolutely," the woman said. Her Texas drawl made Maya smile.

As the woman was adding her name and email address to the guest book, Maya caught sight of the back of the man's head again.

"I hope you can read my terrible handwriting," the woman said. "That's an *o* right there, not an *a*. Can you read that?"

Maya glanced down and read the woman's name. "I can read it just fine. Thank you so much for coming in today, Mrs. Rogers. Please come back soon."

When Mrs. Rogers walked away and the next person stepped up to be helped, Maya asked Meg to take over at the register. Maya made her way through the cluster of people gathered around the shelf with the boxed chocolates. To her surprise, the man was still there. Her heart thudded as she approached him.

"May I help you with something?" She held her breath until he looked up and smiled.

Her heart sank. Of course it was not Ian. She had been crazy to let herself get carried away.

"Hello, Maya," said the man. His familiar greeting startled her. Especially because his words were laced with the hint of an Irish accent. She knew she was imagining things, because his voice sounded like Ian's. So much so that it made goose flesh stand up on her arms. She crossed her arms in front of her and ran her hands over her skin.

"Hello," she said, mustering as enthusiastic a greeting as she could. He was a customer. It wasn't his fault he wasn't the person she had been hoping to see.

The stranger held out his right hand for Maya to shake. "I'm Charles Jordan," he said. "I'm the one who sent you the Facebook message. We communicated back and forth a bit. Oh, or maybe someone else handles the social media for you?"

Maya extended her hand and shook his. "Oh, Mr. Jordan. How lovely to meet you. I am the one who answered your nice note. You said you would be in Texas. I'm so glad that it coincided with the opening of the store. Were you looking for anything in particular?"

He hesitated a moment. Their gazes locked. And there was something in his blue eyes that set loose the butterflies in her stomach.

His voice.

His eyes.

His posture.

It was all uncanny. He reminded her so much of Ian. And it wasn't just because she was wishing that he were there today. For goodness' sake, it had been nearly thirty years since she'd lost him.

Of course, not a day went by that she didn't think of Ian, but it was the rare occasion that she met a man who seemed to be his walking ghost. And even that wasn't right, because other than the eyes, the voice and the way he carried himself, he looked nothing like Ian. Not even Ian aged thirty years.

This man, this Charles Jordan, had a different nose, a different jawline, different cheekbones.

Her gaze fell to the open collar of his blue dress

shirt, where she glimpsed the wide, raised pinkish-white edges of a scar shooting diagonally toward his Adam's apple.

She glanced up. That's when she realized that he was staring at her, too, seeming just as mesmerized. She tore her gaze away, looking toward the shelves.

"We have some lovely gift baskets over here," she said. "And there's still some handmade chocolate left. Not much. I'm pleased to report that it seems to be flying off the shelves."

He was probably just a good soul. The world was full of them, if a person cared enough to look beneath the surface...past the scars. At least that was Maya's philosophy.

"Do you have any Borgia truffles?" he asked. "That's what I had the first time I visited your shop."

Maya's breath caught. *Borgia truffles?*

Borgia truffles had been one of Ian's favorites. The memory made her heart ache.

"No, I'm so sorry. I haven't made those in years. Goodness, probably close to twenty-five years." She'd run into a problem getting the blood-orange extract she used for them. It was only manufactured by one company, and they went out of business. After trying to no avail to find a suitable substitute, she'd finally shelved the recipe.

"I'm so disappointed," he said.

"So it has been a while since you were in the St. Michel shop?" she asked.

"Sadly, it has been much too long. You know how life tends to get in the way. Time goes so fast. Then all of a sudden you realize what's important."

What a strange thing to say.

In an effort to keep things light, Maya replied, "I must say it's quite exciting to say that one of my first customers in my new shop was a return customer from the shop in St. Michel. How about some chocolate-covered salted caramel?"

"That sounds divine," he said.

There it was again. That vague turn of cadence that sounded a bit Irish. But overall he had a decidedly American accent. She motioned for him to follow her to the center of the store so that she could wrap up his caramels.

"Where are you from?"

"All over the place," he answered. "Right now, Orlando, Florida."

"Didn't you say in your message that you are here on business?"

"That I did."

"How long are you in town?"

"Who knows?" He smiled. "Until my business is finished."

Maya knew she shouldn't pry, but she couldn't help herself.

"I must ask, I can't help but think I hear a slight bit of an Irish brogue when you speak. Are you from Ireland, or am I imagining it?"

He gave her a look that seemed to say touché. "That I am. Although I haven't been back in ages. I suppose you can take the boy out of Ireland, but you can't take Ireland out of the boy."

Maya began the process of placing chocolates in a

small box. "How many would you like? A half-dozen? A dozen? That's what I have left."

"I'll take them all."

"Are you enjoying yourself while you're here?"

"I am. I found a great Irish pub downtown. Baldoon's Pub. It feels like home. They even serve your Irish cream chocolate, you know?"

"I do know. It was an arrangement I was excited to make. I'd like to think that it gave the residents of Celebration a preview of what was to come when I opened the shop."

"Well, it seems to have worked."

She felt Charles's gaze on her as she wrapped up his purchase. It made her both excited and a little nervous.

Finally, when she'd finished, she said, "Anything else?"

Charles hesitated a moment. "Would you care to join me for a bite to eat sometime at Baldoon's?"

Maya's immediate reaction was a resounding yes, but caution kicked in before she could get carried away. She didn't know this man who seemed to appear from out of nowhere claiming to have been in her shop twenty-nine years ago.

Even though he reminded her so much of Ian, she had to be careful.

"Oh, goodness, that sounds lovely. However, I don't know when I will have a moment of free time right now. The shop is so new. It requires my constant attention."

Charles Jordan nodded solemnly. "A woman has to eat."

Maya was relieved when Paulina interrupted with a question.

"Excuse me, Maya. I have a customer who has a question that I can't answer. Would you mind helping her? She's in a hurry. She's in here on her lunch hour."

"You'll have to excuse me, please," Maya said to Charles. "Paulina, would you please ring up Mr. Jordan's purchase and have him sign the guest book?"

When she returned about five minutes later, Charles Jordan was gone. He had not signed the guestbook.

Aiden never imagined that a simple shopping trip for something like baby furniture could do so much for a relationship. For that matter, he never thought he'd find himself enjoying shopping so much. Funny how Bia had that effect on him.

The evening he and Bia had spent in Dallas earlier that week, shopping for baby items as if they were a couple, had brought them even closer in a million subtle ways. They were already close, but suddenly there was a new air between the two of them, new life in their relationship. They called each other several times during the day and spent evenings together.

In the past, they may have had dinner together once or twice during the week, and maybe they'd spent a weekend night together if something special was going on. But, of course, both of them had erratic work schedules. Lots of times when he was free, she was working, and vice versa. But when there was a work function, they always seemed to rely on each other as dates. Maybe it was because there had never been any pressure. Maybe it was because they had always enjoyed each other's company.

Now that they were engaged—or *fake engaged,* as Bia kept calling it—spending time together seemed to happen spontaneously, naturally. Spending time with her felt like going home. There was nothing forced or awkward about it. In fact, he'd never enjoyed a woman's company quite so much.

Now they ate dinner together every night. They went for evening walks, after which they would come home and watch movies together sitting side by side on the couch—no more him sitting in the chair and her lounging alone on the couch. Things between the two of them were relaxed and companionable—a phenomenon he had never experienced with anyone else. In the past, he'd always known when he'd spent *too much* time with a woman. He would be bucking for some alone time or time with the guys.

Now things were different.

He didn't know what it all meant, only that it felt good. It felt *right.*

After the *XYZ* spot aired, he didn't feel the need to explain away the engagement to his buddies. Sure, they'd asked, but he hadn't really given them an explanation. Nobody asked about the baby. Funny thing was, they didn't seem to think it was so strange that, all of a sudden, he was engaged to Bia. In fact, his buddy Miles Mercer had said, "It's about damn time you settled down. You two make a great couple."

Of course, Miles was happily married to Sydney James. So his perspective might have been a little bit colored. But he was also a good example of how good being with the right woman could be.

He knew they'd reached a different place in their relationship. They didn't really feel platonic, but it was different than it used to be. He couldn't get a read. He didn't know exactly where they stood or how this would all go down in the end, but that was okay. For now, he was content to let things ride.

There'd been no physical intimacy. Not even another kiss since the one they'd shared in front of the *XYZ* reporter. He had relived that kiss every day, but he wasn't going to risk blowing everything out of the water by trying it again. Still, despite the lack of a physical relationship, he felt closer to her than ever. Of course, she seemed to have her fair share of hormones, or at least that's what she chalked her occasional moodiness up to. But he had decided it would be a challenge to change her mood when she had her moments, and usually he was successful. The place where he really felt he was making the most progress was that she hadn't brought up the trust issues since he'd put the ring on her finger.

All these changes between them had added up to a trial run of what they would be like as a couple, and he hadn't felt the urge to pull away.

For him, that was huge.

Bia had always had a special place in his heart, but now she had taken up residency there. That was the reason he didn't mind spending a Saturday evening putting up shelves in the spare bedroom that would be the baby's room.

She had already started buying things and wanted

to get organized as soon as possible. Even though she wasn't due for another six and a half months, her job demanded a lot of her—a lot of overtime and sometimes unpredictable hours, depending on what she needed to cover for the newspaper.

When she had asked him to put up the shelves tonight, he hadn't hesitated. Toolbox in hand, he walked up the porch steps and let himself inside her house.

"Hi, honey, I'm home!" The one thing in their relationship that remained the same was that they could joke with each other.

"I'm in the baby's room," she called.

He followed her voice down the hall to the first door on the left, where he saw her standing on a stepladder getting something out of the closet.

"Be careful," he said. "Do you want me to do that for you?"

"I'm fine," she said. "But here—could you take this?"

She turned and handed him a medium-size cardboard box she had gotten off the top shelf of the closet. He took it from her, set it on the dresser and extended a hand to help her down from the ladder.

It was a good thing he had because she faltered on the last step and fell into him. He caught her, holding her in his arms.

She didn't say a word and gazed up at him, looking shocked.

"See, this is why you need me," he murmured.

He closed the circle of his arms around her and pulled her closer. He lowered his head toward her, hesitating a moment, giving her a chance to object.

Their first kiss had been for the benefit of the tabloid reporter. Whether they wanted to acknowledge it or not, that kiss had been fueled by temptation and attraction that had been building for years.

It had been a subconscious test. A justified pushing of the envelope to see if their relationship could go there. They had crossed the bridge. And not only had they survived; they seemed to be thriving.

His mouth fused to hers.

This kiss wasn't for show. This one had been a long time coming. Silently she confirmed that, kissing him back, allowing him to take the kiss deeper. She moved against him, sliding her hands up his arms, over his shoulders until her fingers laced around the nape of his neck, holding him.

A hot rush of need coursed through his veins, a need the likes of which he'd never felt before. How was it that each new step they took overwhelmed his senses even more, bringing on new feelings and desires—fiery, fierce and undeniable. Feelings he had never experienced in his long history of women. Because each woman he'd pursued was supposed to be the antidote to his feelings for Bia. Little did he know there was no antidote. There was no way out or around. Only through her could he be happy.

His hands slid down the length of her curves until he cupped her bottom and pulled her closer, reveling in how perfect her body fit against his. She moaned into their kiss.

Keeping one hand in place, the fingertips of the other found the waistband of her shorts and dipped beneath the cloth barrier that stood between them.

Obstacles.

There had always been obstacles between them—
Duane or Hugh or Tracey or some woman he couldn't
feel anything for except a cordial kindness, which always meant cutting her loose before the friendship
outgrew the bounds of amity. Physical distance, engagements, his marriage and jobs had separated them,
too. Until finally the job in Celebration had presented
itself. He had been patient, not wanting to move too
fast when he'd first arrived, because things seemed
to be going well between them. And then there was
Hugh.

Enough was enough.

He was claiming what was his.

Chapter Nine

When she closed the doors to the chocolate shop the end of the first week that it had been open for business, Maya was both exhilarated and exhausted.

Business had been steady the entire week. She was working hard to keep up with the demand—especially for her handmade chocolates. Bia had been in to see her a couple of times. During the last visit, she'd asked if Maya would like to meet Aiden.

Of course she would. Maya had noticed the engagement ring on Bia's hand, but she hadn't asked too many questions other than having Bia confirm that she was, indeed, engaged to be married. There would be plenty of time for details, but right now Maya didn't want to scare her off with too many questions. Even if she was dying to know every last detail of her daughter's life—past, present and future.

It was such a treat to look up from the wrap stand or from a shelf that she had been dusting to see Bia's smiling face. It meant that she was ready for a relationship. Maya could feel it in her bones.

The one person who hadn't returned was Charles Jordan. Perhaps his business in Celebration was finished and he had returned to Orlando before he could say goodbye. Or maybe she had hurt his feelings when she had declined his offer for dinner at the pub.

Whatever the reason for his absence, he had provided an interesting daydream: that somehow Ian was still alive. She needed to stop torturing herself with what could never be and focus on everything that was good in her life.

Even so, on her walk home, she found herself taking a detour. She ended up walking by Baldoon's Pub. While she was down here, she wondered, what could it hurt to pop into the place and check it out? She might even order a shepherd's pie to take home for her dinner.

The place smelled of fried food and beer. It was crowded, but then again it was Saturday night. It was nice to see other downtown businesses thriving.

Maya looked around. She didn't want to sit at the bar. Not alone. But she didn't want to take up a table, either. She was just about to ask the bartender for a menu when a familiar voice behind her said, "Those were the best salted caramels I've ever had in my life." Maya turned around to see Charles Jordan standing there. A strange excitement she hadn't felt in ages blossomed in her stomach. It was a dangerous feeling. She knew she needed to be careful. It wasn't so much that she was in physical danger as it was that her heart might be in jeopardy. She took a long hard look at the tall man clad in khaki pants and a white button-down shirt, his sleeves unbuttoned and pushed up his forearms, his blue eyes and dark hair that was graying at the temples. She saw his broad shoulders, so much like Ian's that it made her want to weep. She found herself a little tongue-tied as heat began to creep up her neck.

"Hello," she said, finally finding her voice. "I thought perhaps you had already returned to Orlando."

"No, I'm still here," he said. "I've been wanting to stop in to see you. However, I thought I'd best pace myself." He patted his middle, but his eyes hinted that he might not be talking about the candy.

"If you call ahead, I will make a fresh batch for you."

Charles nodded. "I'll be sure and do that. In the meantime, would you care to join me for a bite to eat? Seeing that you're already here and all."

He smiled at her, and there was a look in his eyes that pulled her right in.

"That would be lovely," she said and followed him to a table in the middle of the pub.

It had been ages since she had been on a— Would she even call it that? It wasn't a date. She was too traditional to consider this chance meeting a date. She had come here of her own free will to pick up her dinner. She just happened to run into…a friend. Dinner with a friend. That's all this was.

Charles ordered Maya the same ale that he was enjoying.

"How has business been this week?" he asked.

That was a good neutral topic, Maya thought.

"It's been fabulous," she said. "Exhausting, actually. I may have to hire more help if business keeps up at the pace that it was this week. Then again, I suspect some of the customers may have just been curious. I hope they will return. I suppose I'll just have to wait and see."

Charles had propped his elbow on the table and was leaning on his fist, gazing at Maya. His stare made her uncomfortable. It made her want to fill the silence with words. And she usually didn't ramble.

Despite the awkward silence, she forced herself to be quiet.

The server returned with her beer, tried to flirt a little with Charles and then left them alone to look at the menus.

"Do you believe in fate, Maya?" he asked.

What kind of question was that? She'd never really thought about it, although to some extent her life did seem a bit preordained. The chocolate shop had been passed down from one generation to the other. Her stomach fluttered as she thought, for the very first time, that she might now have an heir to continue the legacy. Then again, Bia had her own career. Her daughter had freedom of choice. Fate was not pushing her; it wasn't driving the train.

"That's an interesting question, Mr. Jordan."

"Are you always so formal?"

Maya shrugged. "Charles. Is that better?"

"Much."

"You remind me of someone," she said. "I keep trying to decide if it's because I remember you from your visit to the St. Michel shop. But that was so long ago. I've had many customers since then."

"Who do I remind you of?"

"Somebody from a long time ago."

"Did you care for this person?"

"A great deal." She suddenly caught herself, not sure she wanted to continue where this conversation was headed. "I must say, Charles, you're awfully forward to be asking such personal questions. Questions about fate. Questions about my past. What about your past? Do you believe in fate?"

"I believe that sometimes life puts us in a position where we don't have the luxury of choosing the path that we want to take."

"I'm not exactly sure what you mean by that."

"There's not an easy explanation."

He was looking at her so intensely that for a moment Maya couldn't breathe. Those eyes. Those blue, blue eyes. She'd only seen eyes that color—with flecks of silver and gold radiating from the iris—one other time. If she looked only at his eyes, she felt in her soul that this man was Ian. But that was impossible. She knew it was, and all the hurt that she had managed to shove away over the years sprang free from its trap, lodging in her heart and in the very blood that coursed through her veins.

She couldn't do this to herself. So much was going right in her life right now—the reunion with Bia, the new shop. Why was she going to torture herself with what she couldn't have when things were going so well?

Common sense said that she found Charles Jordan attractive. Why not try to start anew?

Why not? For the same reason she had never been able to love anyone else since the day that she found out Ian was dead. Charles Jordan reminded her of everything that she had loved and lost and would never have again.

It wasn't fair to him.

But what was she supposed to say? *I can't do this because you speak in riddles and remind me of my dead soul mate? Is that all I'm responding to? That you look like somebody who loved me and left me and took my heart with him?*

But you're a stranger who appeared out of nowhere. This just won't work.

"If you'll excuse me for just a moment, I need to—"

She stood up from the table and walked quickly toward the front door.

Bia's life felt fuller with Aiden in it. There was no doubt about that. Or about how these newfound feelings scared her more than just a little bit. All these years, she'd thought she had him figured out, but every day she was learning so many new things.

Every time they were together, she found out something new about him. Small things, such as how he liked pickles but did not like them on his sandwiches. He wanted them on the side. She'd never noticed that before. And that while he liked to tell her about his day, he needed a few minutes after work to unwind and change gears. In the past, they hadn't been around each other in these off hours, and she'd never realized just how much they could reveal about a person. One of the best things she'd recently learned about *bad boy* Aiden Woods was that he called his mother, who now lived in North Carolina, faithfully every Sunday afternoon. He had a deep connection with his family. When he talked about his mother, his sister and her family—they lived in the same small town as his mother—he exhibited a warmth and vulnerability that she never knew he possessed. These were just a few of the things she was beginning to discover and appreciate about him. And the more she learned, the more vulnerable she felt.

They were so natural together, and it didn't feel weird.

And that, in itself, was weird.

Her equilibrium was off, and she couldn't keep blaming it on the pregnancy hormones. She feared she was beginning to buy into the PR that she and Aiden were selling to everyone else, and she wondered if she should start thinking about an escape plan.

Just as Cinderella's ball had ended at midnight, she was beginning to realize that their own bewitching hour would come. How was this fairy tale that they'd spun supposed to end? Because good things always ended. And she needed to start thinking of a plausible way out before her heart got in any deeper.

Everyone knew them as a couple now. However, Aiden's friends and coworkers had mostly stayed out of their business except to offer congratulations. She appreciated the space.

However, tonight was the dinner party at Drew and Caroline's house. Miles and Sydney would be there, along with Pepper and Rob, and another couple—A.J. and her husband, Shane.

Venturing outside the intimate bubble world that she and Aiden had created, she feared that things were about to get really real. As she began to get ready for the party, she wished that she would have declined the invitation.

Nerves flew around her stomach like a swarm of dragonflies. It was the first time she and Aiden would be out as a couple with a group. Now that they were together, they would be invited to gatherings like this dinner party—things that couples did together. In the past, they'd never been included.

It was as if now that they were a couple they were somehow validated. That bothered her a little bit. She had been an interesting person before she had merged with Aiden. And the joke was on the others, since they weren't really a couple at all.

Tonight, they would be thrown together with actual couples, and she hoped it wasn't a recipe for disaster.

Her hair was done. She'd taken extra time with her makeup, and she'd chosen a green sundress paired with strappy sandals bejeweled with rhinestones. The dress, with its V neckline and full skirt, had always made her feel pretty. Now it accentuated the new fullness of her breasts. She paused a moment to appreciate her still slim waistline. All too soon it would be a thing of the past. At least until after she had the baby and could get back into shape.

She had to admit that despite her earlier trepidations, she felt sort of sexy getting all dressed up to go out. If she was completely honest with herself, she would admit that she was eager to see Aiden's reaction when he saw her.

It had been a long time since she'd felt sexy. And, it seemed, even longer since she'd been out on a date. If this even qualified as a date. Despite the rational side of her brain telling her not to make more of this than she should, it felt like a date.

She was at her jewelry box, selecting a simple pair of hoop earrings, when she heard the sound of the front door opening as Aiden let himself in.

"Hello!" he called.

Her heart pounded.

"I'm in the bedroom," she called. "I'll be right out."

She put in her earrings, then gave herself one last once-over in the full-length mirror.

"I have a bottle of merlot to bring with us tonight," Aiden called from the living room. "And a bottle of club soda for you."

He'd remembered the club soda.

Oh, it really did feel like a date.

Insecurity hit her like a tidal wave and threatened to knock her flat. Was the dress too much? Too low-cut?

She tugged at the V-neck.

People were used to seeing her in business attire or simple blue jeans and a button-down. Oh, well, this would be a definite change. She straightened her shoulders and lifted her chin, trying to remember how good she had felt just moments ago.

Ah, well, this would have to do.

Come on, you can do this.

She wanted to do this.

And what about the exit strategy that had sounded like such a good idea before Aiden had arrived with the club soda?

The club soda was for tonight. The exit strategy would have to wait for another day.

She walked out into the living room, her heels click-clacking on the wood floor in a way that made her want to shift her weight to her toes. But she didn't, for fear that she might lose her balance. She'd purchased the sandals on a whim when Hugh had been in town. She'd only worn them once—the night of the Doctor's Ball.

When she'd purchased them, she had been determined to change up her image. It had been a delusional moment, and look where it had landed her.

But the minute Aiden glanced up and saw her, the look on his face made her heart say, *Hugh who?*

His right brow shot up.

Bia's heart pounded, equal parts excitement and nerves.

"Hey, you," he murmured. He stood up, like the Southern gentleman she'd never known he was—yet another new revelation—taking in her appearance with an appreciative glint in his eyes.

She couldn't help but smile. "Hey, yourself," she said, suddenly feeling more like herself again.

It was amazing how he affected her that way. He made her feel appreciated, as if there were no other place in the world he wanted to be and no other person he would rather be with.

But she was no fool; she wouldn't delude herself into believing that he could be exclusively hers forever. Not Aiden. He was already doing so much for her—it wasn't fair to expect that of him.

Of course, when things were going so well the beast of doubt always had to rampage through.

She didn't want to ruin the night. She could confidently say that while she had herself together when it came to business, her love life was another matter altogether. She had a history of making bad choices: trusting Duane, sleeping with Hugh and getting pregnant. She didn't want Aiden to become a casualty of this charade.

As she stood there watching him watching her, she realized that she had been blaming him for the breakup with Duane because it provided a convenient barrier to keep her heart safe. She had made Aiden out to be the bad guy, making herself believe that his was the face of a player, that he was the guy who couldn't stand to see another couple happy—especially after he and Tracey divorced. It was easier to ignore her own feelings for him when she was holding him responsible for her breakup. But after spending so much time with him, after allowing him to kiss her senseless, all the reasons *why not* had fallen away. Her heart was naked and vulnerable with the reality that she had it bad for Aiden Woods.

She who was no prize—pregnant with someone else's child—had lost her heart to a man who could have anyone. And she couldn't afford to keep making bad choices about love because now it wasn't just herself that she had to consider.

She had to think about the baby.

Chapter Ten

The party at Drew and Caroline's house was a co-congratulations affair: congratulations to Bia and Aiden on their engagement and three cheers for a successful grand opening for the new location of Maya's Chocolates.

Maya sat back and watched and listened as her friends talked and laughed around the dinner table, leisurely sipping their wine, Bia sipping her club soda. They were in no hurry to get up. Even though she was the only one without a date, she loved being included, soaking up the positive vibe.

The shop wasn't open on Sundays. So she hadn't seen or talked to Charles Jordan since last night. She felt silly for having bolted on him, but Maya always trusted her intuition and it had been propelling her to leave.

Today, as she thought about it, she realized she hadn't felt in physical danger when she was with him—every nerve in her body was telling her that Charles Jordan was not a dangerous man, or at least not someone who wanted to cause her physical harm.

Heartache, however? That's what scared her.

And it's why she'd run.

She was too busy with the new shop, and the last thing she needed was someone who dredged up heartache to derail her focus.

And she certainly didn't want to think about it tonight.

She shoved Charles Jordan into the recesses of her mind, where he seemed to have taken up permanent residence, and shut the door on him.

The smell of homemade lasagna and garlic bread hung in the air. Even though Maya was stuffed, she savored the aroma. The pasta dish, made entirely from scratch, was a specialty of Celebrations, Inc., Catering, the company owned by Pepper, A.J., Caroline and Sydney.

No wonder their business was so good clients were booking four months in advance.

It warmed her heart to look around the table through the candlelight and see everyone so happy. Successful in business, happy in love. And to think that she'd had a hand in bringing together just about every couple at the table.

Pepper and Rob.

A.J. and Shane.

Caroline and Drew.

Sydney and Miles.

Rob's sister Kate and her new husband were also there. While she hadn't foretold that marriage—not in the same way she had with the other four couples—she'd had the pleasure of serving as the emcee for the bachelor auction where Kate had placed the winning bid for the date with Liam, who was now her husband.

Her gaze drifted to Bia and Aiden.

She'd just met Aiden tonight. He was handsome. A great guy, loving and attentive to Bia. Maya was so pleased when she'd learned that he had proposed to her daughter.

However, something was off.

She couldn't quite put her finger on it, but something between the two of them was different. At least it was different than the vibes between the other couples.

Maybe it was because Bia was her daughter and their relationship was so new? That might skew things.

Tiger Mother syndrome?

No, actually, that wasn't it. She liked Aiden well enough and from what she could discern, he was absolutely smitten with Bia. The downturn was more from Bia.

Hmmm...

Maya hoped that there would be many more opportunities for her and her daughter to spend time together so that they could talk and Maya could try and figure out exactly what was amiss.

The young woman was guarded. While the other girls had popped the corks on bottles of champagne and had fussed over Bia's engagement ring when she and Aiden had first arrived, Bia seemed to hold back emotionally.

Maybe she was simply reserved, the cautious type who didn't wear her heart on her sleeve for everyone to see.... Perhaps. But it felt like there was more to it than that.

Maya could feel it in her bones.

Of course, there was the matter of the baby's paternity, but Aiden knew about that, even if the others didn't. He was marrying her with full disclosure.

Thank goodness everyone at the party had the good grace not to mention the horrid tabloid show and the reporter who was still speculating and lurking around town.

Maya had never seen *XYZ Celebrity News* until Bia had told her about the ambush. Thank goodness she'd watched it, because the guy had shown up in her shop one day asking her employees questions—not about Bia specifically, but he was fishing for information about Hugh Newman—looking for information about the time he had spent in Celebration previously. He had asked if the girls had seen Hugh around and more specifically if they had seen him around town with any women.

Maya had shown the guy the door, threatening to call the police if he didn't leave.

"Who wants dessert?" Caroline asked. "I have red velvet cake and coffee in the kitchen."

Bia stood. "Caroline, let me get dessert. You've worked so hard today having us over. Please relax."

"Yes, Caroline, please do. I am happy to help Bia clear the table and get the dessert."

In a matter of moments, Bia and Maya were in the kitchen slicing the tall red velvet cake that Caroline had made and left on a plate on the island in the center of her kitchen. Maya was doing the cutting and Bia was using a spatula to transfer the delicious-looking cake to dessert plates.

"Aiden is nice," Maya said. "He seems to care for you very much."

Maya glanced up just in time to see a certain look in Bia's eyes that confirmed her earlier suspicion. But as quickly as the emotion flashed, Bia's wall went up and a placid smile masked whatever it was that had initially troubled her.

As soon as Bia had delivered the last piece of cake to the dessert plate, Maya took her daughter's left hand and looked at the ring.

"That's a gorgeous ring," she said. "How did he propose?"

Bia cleared her throat. "He did it the old-fashioned way. He got down on one knee and asked me to be his wife."

"Were you surprised?"

The placid smile transformed into a wry grin. "I can assure you, I have never been more surprised in my entire life."

"But he hadn't given you the ring when the reporter showed up that day harassing you?"

Bia's brow furrowed, and her gaze flicked to the door between the kitchen and the dining room just as a bubble of laughter erupted from the gang.

They were engrossed in another matter and couldn't hear what they were talking about in the kitchen. Bia visibly relaxed.

"No, the day the reporter ambushed me was the first time I heard Aiden refer to me as his fiancée. The ring came later. So, technically, maybe I was a little more surprised that time than when he gave me the ring."

Maya nodded. "I just want to be sure that you're happy."

"I'll be happy when the *XYZ* reporter is gone for good." She lowered her voice to a whisper. "I still haven't found out who tipped him off those two times that he came after me. Has he been back to the shop at all?"

Maya shook her head. "No, I think he knows better than to darken the door of my shop. There's nothing like the protection of a mother who senses her daughter is in danger."

The words hung in the air between them. Bia's expression was unreadable for a moment.

Finally she said, "I appreciate you looking out for me."

Bia set the sugar bowl and cream pitcher on a tray that Caroline had left on another counter. She gestured toward the dining room with her head. "They don't know the other bit of recent happy news, do they? That you're my birth mother. I mean, Aiden knows, of course. But nobody else. Do they?"

"No, they don't."

She stopped what she was doing and turned full attention on Maya. "All that time you were here in Celebration after my father passed away, you didn't tell them that was part of the reason that you were here?"

She'd never really told Bia that's what had initially drawn her here. However, it didn't really take a genius to put two and two together. "No, I didn't want you to hear the news from anyone but me. And I didn't want to tell anyone until I knew you were ready to talk about it."

"I think I'm ready now. Shall we tell them?"

Everyone at the dinner party had seemed even more surprised to learn that Maya was Bia's birth mother than by the news that Bia and Aiden were getting married—scratch that—that they were *engaged.* Of course they'd all had a chance to digest the engagement before the dinner party on Sunday night. So, if they'd been at all shocked by it, they'd managed to mind their manners when they were all together.

The evening had been a nice celebration.

It had happened after Maya and Bia had distributed the cake and coffee. Maya had simply said, "As if we don't have enough to celebrate, there's more good news."

Everyone had quieted down and turned their attention to Maya. "Not many people know this about me, but when I was eighteen years old I met a man who was the love of my life. We had a few happy months together. Then, sadly, he died in a tragic automobile accident. I was pregnant with his child."

Every gaze in the room was riveted to Maya.

"It was a different day and age back then, and since I was from a small provincial town, my mother and grandmother, who both had extremely traditional values, were horrified by my pregnancy out of wedlock. They sent me away to have the baby and arranged for the child—a baby girl—to be adopted by a couple who could not have a child of their own. I grieved the loss of my baby, just as much as I grieved the loss of my soul mate. And even though I knew there was never a chance that I would see my love again, deep in my heart I held out hope that I would be reunited with my child.

"Of course, it was a closed adoption. The adoptive parents were adamant about that. They didn't want to take the chance of me changing my mind. However, my mother had the foresight to ask the agency to give the adoptive parents my information just in case. Whatever she figured might constitute 'just in case,' I will never know. I didn't know then that the parents knew how to find me, only that they had taken my baby girl from me. I thought I would never see her again.

"Then about eighteen months ago, I received a letter from a man informing me that he was the husband of the couple who had adopted my daughter. His wife had passed away years ago. Now he was dying, and he didn't have long to live. He told me that it was his dying wish that his daughter—my daughter—should not be left alone after he died.

"If I had any desire whatsoever to know my daughter, he asked that I wait until after he was gone. But then he would be happy for me to be a part of Bia's life."

Everyone in the room had gasped at the revelation. But they were happy that they could be among the first to share the wonderful news. It was just sinking in that Maya was family. She was Bia's *mother*. It was comforting to know that Maya had not given her up voluntarily. She really hadn't had any choice.

Actually, if you wanted to look for the silver lining, Maya had chosen to give Bia a better life by giving her up to loving parents who desperately wanted a child.

Later that week, Bia pondered the thought as she pulled into a parking place at the grocery store. As she put the car in Park and reached over to turn off the ignition, she glanced down at the dashboard. A yellow warning light that she'd never seen before was illuminated. She took the car owner's manual out of the glove box and looked up the problem.

It turned out to be a bulb failure warning sensor, which meant that somewhere on the vehicle a bulb had blown or was about to.

Thank goodness it didn't seem to be anything serious. Aiden was working late and Maya was coming over for dinner tonight. Bia would ask him about it tomorrow. If it was something simple, she'd see if he could show her how to change it. If not, she could take it to the dealership.

She fished her shopping list out of her purse, got out of the car and locked it before walking into the store.

At the party, A.J. had given her a couple of recipes that sounded delicious: soy ginger–glazed salmon and Asian coleslaw. She was making them for dinner tonight. She was trying to be so careful about eating healthy for the baby. She figured salmon was a good choice. Plus, it would be quick and easy to put on the table.

Since it was something not in her usual recipe repertoire, she didn't have many of the ingredients on hand. It was okay; she was learning it was a good thing to try new things every once in a while. Her mind drifted to Aiden. This phase in their relationship was definitely something new. It felt as if she was walking out on a glass bridge. Her senses kept preparing her for a crash landing. Yet she was fine—something sturdy and unseen was holding her up. If she didn't look down, she just might be all right.

She needed to keep reminding herself of that. Or maybe she should just quit thinking about it altogether. Quit overthinking and live.

She was in the aisle with the cooking oils, searching for sesame oil, when she heard a voice behind her.

"Well, if it isn't Bia Anderson," the woman said.

Bia flinched inwardly before she turned around and saw a woman that Aiden had dated on and off for a couple of months. She had only met the woman one time, and she didn't remember her name. It was something like Judy…or Julie…or Juliet?

"Hello," Bia said vaguely, still racking her brain for the woman's name. There had been so many women, it was hard to keep track. Actually, she hadn't catalogued them, but this one was so pretty she stood out from the bunch. Tall, blonde and model-thin. Bia swallowed a pang of…what? Jealousy? Inadequacy?

"I'm Joanna," she said. "You probably don't re-member me. But I'm Aiden's old…um…Aiden and I used to…um…"

"I do remember you, Joanna. Yes, you and Aiden used to date. It's nice of you to say hello."

The woman with her Heidi Klum looks was perfect. If Aiden didn't want her, Bia didn't understand what he was looking for. If she wasn't good enough… Well.

"I understand congratulations are in order. I wanted to get a good look at the woman who finally snagged Aiden Woods's heart. May I see the ring?"

These words coming from tall, beautiful Joanna took Bia aback. Bia held up her hand, and, as the woman studied it, Bia had a chance to study her per-fect complexion, her wide-set blue eyes and other clas-sic features.

Good God, Aiden. If this woman isn't good enough for you, what in the world do you want?

Then Bia recognized the feeling she was fighting. It was regret. She certainly couldn't compete with Joanna. The escape plan that she'd been thinking so much about…she needed to get to work on that.

"It really is gorgeous," Joanna said wistfully. "It's just the kind of ring I knew Aiden would pick out."

Bia's expression must have betrayed her.

"Oh, honey, you don't have to worry about me. I tossed in the Aiden towel months ago. But I have to warn you, Lisa English is devastated. You might want to watch your back there. She's not going away with-out a fight."

Watch my back?

Was she kidding?

Joanna gave Bia a once-over that ended with a patronizing smile. It could have been described as pity.

"Good luck, Bia." The words *you're going to need it* went unsaid, but they hung in the air, as heavily as Joanna's perfume, after she turned and click-clacked her way down the aisle.

Chapter Eleven

An hour later, standing in her kitchen, Bia took out her angst on the green, red and napa cabbage, shredding it for the coleslaw and trying not to get sucked into a black hole of doubt.

The grocery store rendezvous with Joanna had been a huge reality check for Bia. The problem with being a realist was that she refused to delude herself. She and Joanna were two completely different breeds of women. And if Aiden didn't want Joanna…

Bia blinked away the nagging thought and reread the recipe, which called for slicing carrots into ultra-thin matchsticks. She focused on making each cut as precise and uniform as she could.

She was good at things like this—checking newspaper stories for grammar and fact. Following recipes and slicing vegetables into precise matchstick pieces. Logical things. Things that took precision and concentration. These were the things she had control over. This was her comfort zone, and that's where she was confident. But she had no more desire to put herself out there on the dating scene, head-to-head with women like Joanna and this Lisa English—whoever she was—than she wanted to get up onstage and try to outsing Christina Aguilera.

Joanna and Lisa were the type of women Aiden was attracted to. Beautiful, fashionable, trophy girlfriend material. That's exactly what they were. What the heck was wrong with Aiden?

Bia stopped cutting, realization creeping over her.

Aiden dated these women until they fell for him. Was he only into the thrill of the chase? He pursued women until they wanted him and then he got the heck out of Dodge…as fast as he could. It had even happened with Tracey after they'd gotten married.

Huh.

The symptoms sure did seem to fit the disease.

Maybe the chance meeting with Joanna was a good reminder that Bia needed to not get carried away. Even though kissing Aiden felt pretty darn right, she needed to take off the *lurve* goggles and see the situation for what it really was.

But for some reason, that didn't sit right with her, either.

Bia had just put the salmon in the oven when Maya arrived. She remembered what Maya had said that first day she had come to interview her: that Bia had already met the love of her life. That he was in her life, and all she needed to do was appreciate what was right in front of her.

Against Bia's better judgment, the completely senseless heart of her that she never allowed to have a voice was speaking up loud and clear: somehow, some way she wished that person could be Aiden.

Who else could it be?

And here she was talking to herself as if she believed in Maya's *woo-woo* proclamations.

All she had to lose was her heart. But before she could do that, she needed to know that she and the baby were safe. That she wasn't making another colossal mistake.

Maya greeted Bia with a big warm hug and what looked like a box of chocolates.

"Come in!" said Bia.

"I can't even begin to tell you how much I've been looking forward to this evening," Maya said. "These are for you."

Bia gratefully accepted the chocolates. "These will make a fabulous dessert. Thank you."

"I hope I'm not late," Maya said. "I came straight from work. But it took longer than I thought it would to close up shop for the day. I suppose I could have let the staff do it, but we're still getting used to each other."

"I'm sure that will happen in no time," Bia said. "But you're not late. I just put the salmon in the oven. Would you mind coming into the kitchen? I'm still working on another dish for dinner."

Bia noticed the way that Maya glanced around as she walked toward the kitchen. She seemed to be tak-

ing in all the details of her house. It was the first time
Maya had ever been there. She tried to see the place
through Maya's eyes: the living room with the big,
overstuffed red sofa; the rustic plank wood coffee
table with several magazines fanned out, a grouping
of candles and a silk orchid plant that looked real; an
entertainment center with a flat-screen TV. It was all
her own furniture that she'd moved in from her apartment after her father had passed away. The only thing
of his that remained was his old recliner, which was in
dire need of reupholstering, and some of the paintings
and family photos that still hung on the wall. While
she'd done her best to make the house that she'd grown
up in her own, she couldn't bring herself to part with
those remnants of the past.

"You have such a nice home," Maya said.

"Thank you. I grew up in this house. Lived here
all my life except for the years I was away at college
and in my apartment when I came back to take the
reporting job at the paper."

Maya walked over to the fireplace and picked up a
frame that contained one of the few family portraits
they'd had taken before Brenda, Bia's adoptive mom,
had died.

"How old were you here?" Maya asked.

"I was three."

"Look at you with your red curls. You're such a
beautiful child. You still are."

Bia smiled her thanks at the motherly comment.

She paused in the doorway, watching Maya set
down the picture and glance around again, seemingly
taking everything in.

"I'm just trying to imagine you as a three-year-old running around this house."

"Do you have any regrets?" Bia asked. "I mean, I know you were in no position to care for a child, especially since your family wasn't very supportive of your situation, but…"

As the words left her mouth, it struck Bia as odd that a family that had prided itself on passing a business down from one generation to another would be so willing to give up one of their own. Maybe they thought Maya would have other children.

Oh, well.

That was a long time ago, and Bia could read the sorrow in Maya's eyes.

"If I could do it over again, I would do it differently," she said. "But I'm a firm believer in not staining the present with regrets over the past." She took a deep breath, exhaled and smiled. "I always knew that I would see you again. I always clung to that belief. Now look at us. Here we are."

"Yes. Here we are."

This was her mother.

Her *mother.* Even though it had taken a while to wrap her mind around the fact that her father had kept the truth about her birth from her for all those years, he had been instrumental in bringing the two of them together.

As they made their way into the kitchen, Bia thought about how sometimes you had to look past the first impression to realize the beauty in something that at first glance might seem devastating.

"I just realized I've never asked you where you

live," Bia said as she busied herself measuring out ingredients for the coleslaw dressing.

"I have a small studio on the second floor of the shop."

Bia glanced up from her recipe. "I didn't even realize that the shop had a second story."

"It's more of a renovated attic space. But I have a nice full bathroom and a place to sleep. Actually, it's quite cozy. The best part is, I can't beat the commute."

The two of them laughed at Maya's joke, then exchanged stories and snippets of information, bringing each other up-to-date with their lives with broad brushstrokes covering the missing years. She really was happy to have this time with Maya...her mother.

The reality of it made her catch her breath each time she thought about Maya being her mother. At least, for the most part, it kept her mind off the Joanna incident. Occasionally, her mind would drift back to their conversation in the grocery store, but Bia would force herself to think about something else. She thought she was doing a pretty good job keeping a sunny disposition.

Still, somehow Maya seemed to see through the facade. "Is everything all right?"

Bia tossed the cabbage in the dressing. "Of course. Why do you ask?"

"You just don't seem like yourself tonight. Are you feeling all right?"

Bia nodded. "I guess I'm just a little bit tired. We just put this week's edition of the paper to bed last night. It always takes a lot out of me to get that done."

"Please let me help you with the rest of dinner," said Maya.

"It's a very simple meal," Bia said. "It's almost done. So, just have a seat and relax. You must be tired, too, after being on your feet all day."

"Well, if you won't let me help you with the cooking, while you do that, I'll set the table for you."

"That would be fabulous. And would you please put on the kettle for some herbal tea? I'd love some with dinner, but would you like a glass of wine?"

"Tea sounds perfect."

Bia showed Maya the drawer with the silverware and pointed out a basket of cloth napkins.

"Is Aiden joining us tonight?"

Bia inhaled sharply. The mention of his name had caused her stomach to do a little somersault. Oh, that wasn't good. She needed to stop doing things like that. She needed to stop remembering the feel of his lips on hers and the way his hands had taken possession of her body.

"No, he's working tonight. It's just you and me."

"Are you missing him?" Maya asked. "Is that why you seem a little blue?"

Bia threw a quick glance over her shoulder at Maya, who was fishing the silverware out of the drawer.

"Well, no. I wouldn't say that exactly."

Maya walked up and placed a hand on Bia's shoulder and gave a little squeeze.

Bia made a conscious effort to relax. "I think my hormones are knocking me for a loop. I don't know what's wrong with me."

"What do you mean?"

"I was at the grocery store after I got off work, and I ran into an old girlfriend of Aiden's."

Maya looked at her quizzically. "Did she upset you?"

"Yes, but it's not her fault."

"What did she do?"

Nothing. She didn't do anything. How did she tell Maya that the only thing the woman was guilty of was being gorgeous and dating Aiden?

Bia knew she was being ridiculous without even saying the words. It was the hormones. Was it the hormones that were bothering her? Or was it the fact that she wasn't telling the truth? Right now she wanted nothing more than to talk to Maya.

"May I confide in you?" Bia asked.

"This engagement isn't real. Aiden has agreed to do this to help me out."

Bia explained everything to Maya—how Aiden had spontaneously jumped to her rescue, and, while it was a quick fix for the moment, it had left them in a precarious position. It left Bia vulnerable to the media discovering that she was carrying Hugh's baby.

"We just need to give it some time. Until I'm sure that the tabloid reporters have gone away and aren't planning any more sneak attacks. We've talked about keeping this up until they decide what to do about the movie that Hugh was supposed to be in. Whether they will still shoot in Celebration or if they put the project on hold. Until then it seems pretty certain that the *XYZ* correspondents will be lurking."

Maya didn't look as surprised as Bia thought she

might upon hearing the news. She simply nodded and drew some water for the kettle, ignited the burner on the gas range and set the water to boil.

Bia took down her grandmother's china teapot and two cups and set them on a tray. She put four teaspoons of loose tea leaves into the pot.

"The two of you have been putting on a convincing show," Maya said as she set the table. "From the ring all the way down to the way he looks at you. The energy is right between the two of you. Whether you realize it or not, there is something special here. He's in love with you. Everyone can see it's so. Why are you making this so difficult?"

Bia flinched at the unexpected question.

"What makes you so sure that this energy, as you put it, is right? And what makes you think I am the one who is making this difficult?"

"Because I sense that you are the one who is holding back. How can you expect things to work out if you won't allow him to love you?"

"It's not that easy. I wish it were."

"Falling in love can be the easiest or the most difficult thing in the world. It all depends on what you make of it."

The teakettle whistled, and Maya got up to pour the boiling water into the teapot. As she stood over the steeping pot, she said, "You don't like to be out of control, do you?"

"Does anyone?" asked Bia. "I'm sure if a person could choose to be in control of her life and feelings or not, she would choose to be. Right?"

Maya brought the tray over to the table.

"Anytime a person falls in love, she feels vulnerable and out of control. It's much easier if you just go with it. Don't fight it."

Maya sat down across the table from Bia and poured tea into each of the cups.

"I wish it were that easy," Bia said.

"It's only as hard as you make it," said Maya. "You have to trust Aiden. You have to trust yourself."

"I guess that's the problem. Trust and I...we have a rather complicated relationship."

"Has he given you any reason not to trust him?" Maya asked.

Bia thought back to that night so long ago—the night of the bachelor party—and all the times in between that they'd talked about it. All the years she'd so desperately wanted to pin the blame on someone other than Duane. If she could, then maybe that meant that she hadn't been the one who'd made the mistake. But Aiden was right. The only one to blame was Duane.

"I used to think so," Bia said. "But no. Aiden has been nothing but wonderful to me. He's the one who came up with this plan to protect me. My problem is, I don't want it to ruin our friendship."

Maya sipped her tea thoughtfully. "Why would it?"

Bia told her about her newfound theory. That Aiden was only intrigued by the thrill of the chase.

"And you say this because he has dated a lot of women?"

Bia nodded. "A lot of beautiful women."

"You do realize that he ended things with each of them because they weren't the right women for him?

Otherwise he would be married and we wouldn't be having this conversation."

"Well, he was married once," Bia said.

Maya's brows shot up. "What happened?"

"I don't know. They got a divorce. He won't talk about it. They were married for a couple of years after college, when Aiden was living in Los Angeles."

"He will tell you in good time. Especially after the two of you are married."

"I don't think this will end in marriage," Bia said. "He made an impulsive action. I appreciate it, but I won't hold him to it."

Maya gave her a look like she wasn't convinced.

"You need to talk to him about it," Maya said. "Just be open about how you feel."

How could she be honest with him when she wasn't sure she could even be honest with herself about how she felt?

Thank goodness the stove's timer dinged, indicating that the salmon was finished and that line of the conversation was over. Bia got up to take the fish out of the oven.

While Bia was plating the meal, Maya didn't push the issue any further. That was a good thing, because Bia didn't want to talk about it anymore.

Still, she thought, as she retrieved the slaw from the refrigerator, it was nice to have Maya in her life. Someone to talk to. Despite all the years they'd been apart and the short time that they'd known each other, she felt incredibly connected to Maya. For that, Bia was grateful.

As Bia set a plate in front of Maya, her mother

smiled up at her. A feeling of gratitude washed over Bia in an unexpected wave.

"We've been talking about me all night," Bia said as she took her seat across the table from Maya. "It's your turn."

Maya gave a reticent one-shoulder shrug, dipping her head at Bia's suggestion. "There's not much else to say. I've told you most everything."

Maya took a bite of salmon and chewed it.

"You told me everything?"

Maya swallowed her bite and looked at Bia as if she was contemplating something. "This is delicious, by the way."

"Thank you, but don't change the subject," Bia said. "We're talking about you."

"There might be one thing that I haven't told you. A turn of events that has happened just since I've been in Celebration."

Bia leaned forward. "Is this about a man?"

Maya's left eyebrow arched and a sly smile spread across her face. "Maybe."

"There's no maybe about it," Bia said. "Either there's a man or there's not. Which is it?"

"Okay, so it's about a man. I'm just not sure how he figures. He scares me a little."

Bia's eyes widened. "As in fearing for your safety or he makes you feel vulnerable?"

"I don't know. Okay, I guess he doesn't make me fear for my safety, but I don't know him. He knows me, though. He sent me a message before the store opened saying he'd been to the shop in St. Michel. He's in town on business and…"

Bia propped her elbow on the table and rested her chin on her palm. "And?"

Maya answered her with another shrug.

"All right, Ms. You-Have-to-Be-Willing-to-Be-Vulnerable, I believe it's time you practice what you preach."

Maya laughed. "It's so much easier to give advice than it is to practice it."

Bia looked up at the ceiling. "Finally, my mother understands me."

They both laughed, and Maya told Bia about Charles, about how he had stopped by the shop on opening day and about how she had run out on him at the pub.

"Why does he make you so nervous?"

Suddenly Maya's face turned very solemn. "Because he reminds me of your father. Ian Brannigan was the only man I've ever loved. I haven't been able to feel anything for a man since I lost him."

"Until now?"

"I don't know. I don't know what I feel."

"I hear you. This vulnerability business isn't all it's cracked up to be, is it?"

"Not when you're the one sitting in the seat of vulnerability."

"Will you tell me about my father?" Bia asked. "I would love to know about him."

Maya's trademark placid smile returned to her face. A light the likes of which Bia had never seen on her mother's face ignited as she began to tell the story of how she fell in love with Ian. It dimmed as she recounted how he left one day and never came back, leaving her pregnant with his child, how she eventually learned of his accident.

"He never knew about you. I couldn't imagine him just running off without a goodbye. But when he didn't come back, I thought the worst. I was so mad at him for a long time, for breaking all his promises. He told me he would love me forever and then he just disappeared. The more I thought about it, the more it didn't make sense. It didn't seem like him. But then my mother sent me away and you were born. After I got home I got this crazy idea that I was going to find him. That once he knew about you, he would come back and we would be a family.

"So I called his family, and that's when I learned of the tragic news. It was like losing him all over again, only far worse and much more painful than I could ever imagine. It took me years to be able to smile again—and even then I might've just been going through the motions. I was dead on the inside until I got the letter from your adoptive father and there was the possibility of reuniting with you. My daughter."

Maya reached across the table and took Bia's hand in hers. "For the first time in decades, I am happy, truly happy. So I don't know if these feelings for Charles are an offshoot from the joy I am feeling from our reunion. These similarities that I see in him, the mannerisms, the turns of speech that remind me of your father might just be transference—my wanting to imagine your father here. That's why I need to be careful."

"From what you said, though, Charles sounds like a nice guy. Why not give him a chance?"

Maya pursed her lips and her left brow shot up. Bia was beginning to notice that as one of Maya's trademark expressions.

"I'll make a deal with you," Maya said. "If you give Aiden a chance, I'll consider doing the same with Charles Jordan. Do we have a deal?"

Chapter Twelve

The *Catering to Dallas* shoot wrapped at about nine-thirty, and Aiden was at Bia's house by ten-fifteen. He was surprised to see the yellow Volkswagen convertible in her driveway, but then he remembered that Maya was coming over to have dinner with Bia tonight.

The two women were standing in the foyer when Aiden walked in. They stopped in the middle of what they were saying, looking a little startled to see him.

"Hello," he said. He kissed Bia on the cheek and felt her tense and pull away from him ever so slightly. He took a step back, giving her a quizzical look. "I hope I'm not interrupting."

Maybe he should've knocked, but he and Bia had an open-door policy. Neither of them ever knocked when they entered the other's place. Especially not lately.

"No, you're not interrupting," said Bia. "I'm glad to see you."

Her words said welcome, but her actions were cool and distant.

"Maya and I were just talking about the chocolate business. She is going to show me how to make chocolate. Doesn't that sound like fun?"

"Yes, I am," Maya said a little too brightly.

That may have been the plan, but Aiden got the feeling that's not what they had been talking about when he had walked in. That was fine; they had a lot to catch up on considering all the years they'd been apart. Aiden was glad that Bia had Maya to lean on during the pregnancy. Every woman deserved to have her mother there when she went through life's rites of passage.

"I made salmon for dinner," Bia said. "It's in the oven. I kept it warm for you. Unless you're absolutely starving, I'll fix you a plate after I say goodbye to Maya. If you are starving, go ahead and help yourself."

"Thank you," he said. "You take your time. I can fix my plate. It was good to see you, Maya. Hope to see you again soon."

"Yes," she said. "I hope so, too. I appreciate the way you're taking such good care of Bia. I know she does, too."

Aiden glanced back and saw a funny look wash over Bia's face. Had they been talking about him when he arrived? What was there to say?

"Take care," he said, leaving them alone in the foyer.

"There's coleslaw in the refrigerator," Bia called after him.

He felt like an interloper until he found the foil-covered plate of salmon in the oven. They had talked about him coming over after work, and the dinner proved that she had been expecting him. Still, something didn't feel right.

He heard the front door close, and a moment later Bia was standing in the kitchen with her hands clasped in front of her. She looked so damn sexy in shorts that showed off her long shapely legs and a V-neck top that hinted at just the slightest bit of cleavage. It was almost as if Bia was not aware of it. She obviously wasn't aware of the effect she had on him. For as long as he'd known her, she'd never purposely dressed sexy. That was what made her so alluring. She had a quiet confidence that did more for his libido than if she would have gone for the obvious too-short, too-low-cut getup that so many women favored these days. In his book, subtle was way sexier than in-your-face.

He got the coleslaw and dished it onto his plate. "This looks so good. Thanks for making it for me. I'm starving. We filmed at a wedding reception tonight, and the food smelled incredible. But everything was so chaotic that I didn't get a chance to eat."

He recovered the bowl with plastic wrap and put it back in the refrigerator. "Besides, I wanted to save my appetite for tonight."

Realizing how that might have sounded like a double entendre—he'd actually meant it as one—he glanced over at Bia to gauge her reaction. There was that strange look again.

"What's wrong?" he asked.

She stood there for a moment, looking a little vulnerable. Aiden waited for her to answer.

"I ran into your good friend Joanna at the grocery store this afternoon," Bia said.

"Joanna Brandt?"

"I'm not sure what her last name is. The tall blonde you dated a few months ago."

"I don't know if you'd actually call it dating—"

Bia crossed her arms and furrowed her brow. "You see, that's what I'm talking about. Why did *she* think you were dating if you weren't?"

"What are you talking about?"

Okay. Maybe that's what Bia and Maya had been discussing when he'd walked in. He didn't give Bia a chance to answer.

"How is Joanna?" Aiden said. "I haven't seen her in several months."

"Gorgeous as ever," Bia said. "But, sorry to say, she seems to be over you. She says she threw in the Aiden towel a long time ago, but somebody named Lisa is still hot on your trail."

Lisa?

"Lisa who?" he asked, racking his brain, trying to call forth the face.

"Is there more than one Lisa?" Bia asked. "This one's name is Lisa English. Ring a bell?"

"Lisa English? I never even went out with her. She's a friend of Joanna's. Did Joanna tell you I dated Lisa?"

"Let's see if I can remember what she said." Bia put a finger on her chin and looked up at the ceiling as if she were trying hard to remember. "I think it was something to the tune of, 'I have to warn you, Lisa English is devastated that you and Aiden are engaged. You might want to watch your back there. She's not going to go away without a fight.' Yes. That's what she said. This, of course, came after Joanna said she wanted to get a good look at the woman who'd finally stolen Aiden Woods's heart. You should've seen the look on her face when I told her not to worry—that you were still on the market and that this was all just a big farce."

Aiden nearly choked on his dinner. "What? Did you really say that?"

Bia cocked her head to one side, holding his gaze. "Of course not. I'm not stupid."

"I didn't say you were. I just know that Joanna can be a little…"

Bia had her elbow on the table; her chin rested in her palm. She arched a brow at him and moved her head ever so slightly as if saying, *A little what?*

Was she jealous? Aiden's heart gave a little tug at the possibility. If she was jealous that meant she cared. All those years Bia had stood back as he brought different women around—of course, none of them were anything other than friends to him. Except for Tracey. He'd ended up eloping to Vegas with her. She was the biggest mistake of his life.

Bia had never shown the slightest indication that she was bothered by any of the women. Of course, she was a decent woman—she never would have said anything bad about any of them.

Plus, she had been engaged to Duane all that time.

"Joanna can be a little *persistent,*" he finally said. "She has a very strong personality."

"And you think that I'm not strong enough to stand up to her?"

Oh, boy. This was going downhill fast. If he wasn't careful, he was going to dig himself into a hole.

"I'm sure you can hold your own with Joanna or anyone who puts you in an uncomfortable position."

"Which is why you had to jump in and tell the *XYZ* guy that we were engaged? Because I can handle anyone who puts me in an uncomfortable position?"

Aiden set down his fork. "I didn't come here to fight with you, Bia. I'm sorry you ran into Joanna. I'm sorry she said what she said. But the truth is, I've dated lots of women. I'm not dating them now. I can't change the past, and actually I don't want to. Because the one thing I learned from dating all those women is that none of them was right for me. They weren't you."

She stared at him with big eyes. For a moment, she looked a little disoriented. He feared she might get up and walk away. But he'd said it. Said the thing he'd wanted to say since the first time he'd realized he was in love with her. As he waited for her to say something, he looked down at his hands, which were balled into fists in his lap. He consciously relaxed them.

"Aiden, do you think that's because I'm just about the only woman who doesn't find you irresistible?"

Ouch. Not exactly the response he was hoping for. But something in her eyes went counter to the words that were so confidently flowing from those lips that drove him crazy.

His gaze fell to her mouth.

"Is that the truth, B? You don't feel anything for me? Nothing at all? You could just get up and walk away? From us?"

She inhaled sharply.

"Aiden, there isn't an us, not in the terms that you're talking about. I'm trying to keep us from making a big mistake and ruining everything."

He leaned in. "So, you're saying that you do feel something? Otherwise there wouldn't be any reason for you to need to worry about us. To walk away from us."

She got up and took his plate to the sink. Turned on the faucet, rinsed it and put it in the dishwasher.

He walked up behind her and put his hands on her shoulders. She stiffened but didn't pull away. He leaned in close and whispered in her ear.

"You see, I think the big mistake would be not admitting that there is something here…between us." He kissed her earlobe and then trailed kisses down her neck. She relaxed and leaned back into him, moving her head to the side, allowing him better access. "There's been something brewing between us for a very long time. Tell me that's not true, that you don't feel it, too, and I'll walk away."

He nipped at her earlobe, ran his lips over the tender spot where her ear met her neck. Her breathing became heavy and she seemed to stifle a little moan.

But suddenly she pulled away and looked up at him, her eyes dark with need. "It's not that I don't feel anything for you," she said.

Those lips that he'd longed to taste again were

inches away from his. All he had to do was lean in and claim them.

"I'm the only woman who has ever said no to you. I'm just afraid that once you do get what you want, it will be the end of *us*. I'm afraid that you don't really want me, Aiden. You just want what you can't have."

She stood and looked at him. She was so close that they were breathing the same air. She looking at him with an expression that made him want to pull her in close. To show her just how wrong she was about him.

"Did it ever dawn on you that maybe I've dated so many women because I was trying to get you out of my system?"

"No, that's not true," she said.

Her breath smelled vaguely like peppermint and chocolate and he couldn't help himself; he leaned in and dusted a feather-soft kiss on her bottom lip.

"It is true," he murmured. "That's why no other relationship has lasted. I married Tracey because I thought that might be the best way to get over you. But you know how it turned out."

Bia ducked out of his arms. "No, I don't—not other than the obvious. That the two of you divorced. You never told me. Are you saying you didn't love her, but you married her, anyway?"

Aiden crossed his arms and leaned one hip against the counter. "That's not really a fair question."

"It is, Aiden." She grabbed a rag and started wiping down the countertops. "It's a very fair and straightfor-ward question. Did you love Tracey or not?"

This was a no-win situation. "She divorced me, B. So whether or not I loved her is a moot point."

Bia shook her head and smirked at him as if she'd drawn her own conclusion.

"What about you and Hugh?" He held up a hand. "No, wait—don't answer that. It's a rhetorical question. The only reason I brought it up is because you had your reasons for Hugh. I'm not judging you, and I never will. It happened, but it's in the past and that's where it will stay. I just wish you'd give me the same latitude."

She'd stopped cleaning. She was looking at him now with a softer, if not somewhat conflicted, expression.

"I've been up front with all the women I've dated. I've never cheated or promised them something I had no intention of delivering. They were a part of my past just like Duane and Hugh are a part of yours."

He took a step toward her.

"I just need to know that I can trust you. I have more to think about than just myself now. I mean, I'm pregnant with another man's child, Aiden. That's a lot to ask you to take on. And as much as I would love to try on this—this—this…whatever it is that's happening between us—I'm not in the position to test-drive a relationship and potentially make another mistake. What if we take that next step and it turns out terribly? What if we end up hating each other?"

"I could never hate you, B. Give me a chance. Give *us* a chance."

He took another step toward her, and she didn't move away.

"Just tell me you don't want this as much as I do

and I'll never bring it up again. Just say the word and I'll walk away."

She bit her bottom lip, but she didn't say it.

He drew her into his arms and held her, breathing in that familiar floral coconut scent that was so her. She melted into him.

"Stay with me tonight," she said.

He picked her up and carried her into the bedroom.

Chapter Thirteen

There was proving a point, and then there was proving a point. Aiden had stayed. They'd made out like a couple of teenagers and then they'd fallen asleep in each other's arms.

That's as far as it went. It was all very innocent.

He said he wanted her to believe it wasn't just the thrill of the chase. That even though he wanted her so badly it was all he could do to contain himself, he wanted her to believe that his intentions were honorable.

He was not just out to love her and leave her.

Huh.

For a long, heated while, Bia thought that it wasn't *her* virtue that was about to be compromised—she told him he was the one who should be worried.

Yes. The chemistry that had always zinged between them had more than surpassed expectations once they took it to the bedroom. She could hardly wait to see what it would be like to make love to Aiden.

But they were taking it slowly.

With her propensity to get carried away in the moment, in the light of day, playing it safe seemed like a very good idea.

She was sitting at her dressing table finishing her makeup before work when Aiden brought her a cup of decaf coffee.

"Thank you," she said, smiling up at him.

He set the cup down and enfolded her in a hug. "I loved waking up with you this morning. I want to wake up with you every morning."

A spiral of need coursed in her lady parts.

"If you're not careful," she said. "I'm going to drag you back to that bed and have my way with you."

He answered with a deep openmouthed kiss that she felt all the way to her toes. He slid his hands down the vee of her robe and cupped her breasts. A moan laced with all the pent-up want for him escaped.

"What are you doing to me?" she asked, her lips still on his.

He bit her bottom lip. "I'm proving that you can trust me."

Her hand found his desire straining the front of his button-fly jeans. "Oh, wow, I think we need to figure that out pretty quick. Otherwise, I'm afraid we might spontaneously combust thanks to all this…restraint."

"And how," he said, trailing kisses between her

breasts, up her neck and then finishing with a long, lingering promise of things to come on her lips.

"You're going to be late for work if we keep this up," he said.

"That's why it's good to be the boss," she said into his ear.

"To be continued," he said, fixing her robe, covering her up and returning her to her original unravaged state. "But in the meantime, take my truck to work and I'll find that problem that's setting off the sensor in your car."

"Thanks, but don't you have to work today?"

"I do, but we have a later call time because of how late the shoot went last night."

Thirty minutes later, she was on her way to the office and already thinking about coming home and spending another night in Aiden's arms. She wanted to trust him in the worst way.

She thought about what Maya had said last night about taking chances and allowing yourself to be vulnerable. She had a point—a great point—but opening herself up, leaving her heart so exposed and taking the chance of losing this man who was her best friend in the world was such a scary thought.

But then she thought about Maya coming all this way, setting up a business to be near her daughter without knowing how Bia would react, whether she would accept or reject her.

What if Maya hadn't been open to making herself vulnerable?

They both would've lost out on one of the most beautiful relationships—mother and daughter.

Bia smiled at the thought.

She pulled over to the curb and took out her phone to text Maya: I put myself out there. I expect to hear that you've done the same with CJ.

She added a heart icon and pressed send.

The message sailed off into cyberspace, leaving Bia with a warm, giddy feeling. She had just texted her mother for the first time.

She'd spent the night with Aiden, in a manner of speaking, for the first time, texted her mother for the first time. What other firsts were coming her way? Her body responded with a longing that she felt all the way down to her toes.

All in good time. For now, she was going to let Aiden prove his point, that it wasn't all about the thrill of the chase.

Her phone sounded the arrival of a new text. It was from Maya. Well done. I will have an update from my end later today. Stay tuned.

How fun. Having Maya in her life was better than just having a girlfriend to share her secrets with. She had a mother and a friend all in one.

She was about to text back a reply when her phone died. *Huh.* Last night she'd been so swept away, she'd forgotten to plug in her phone.

The memory made her tingle all over.

She could still feel Aiden's lips on her neck this morning. That made her body sing.

Since Aiden's truck was a newer model, she figured the charger was probably in the console or the glove box. She tried the glove box first. When she opened it, a bundle of papers fell out. They'd fallen far enough out of her reach that she had to leave them on the floor after she plugged her phone into the charger.

When she parked at work, she bent down and retrieved them. She was just about to shove them back into the glove box when something caught her eye. The document was a rider to Aiden's homeowner's insurance policy covering a diamond engagement ring.

A fifteen-thousand-dollar diamond engagement ring.

She glanced at the two-carat sparkler on her left ring finger. For a moment she couldn't breathe. She feared a full-blown panic attack was setting in.

The ring was real?

She thought back to what he'd said when she'd asked him if the ring was real: "Sure, I have an extra fifteen grand lying around. I figured you were worth it."

She felt so stupid. She really had thought it was a spectacular piece of cubic zirconia. It was so much bigger and more sparkly than the modest half-carat ring Duane had given her.

Until now, the ring Duane had given her was the nicest piece of jewelry she'd ever owned.

Fifteen thousand dollars?

The ring felt hot and heavy on her hand. Why would Aiden spend so much on it?

Unless he really was serious?

Oh, my God. Is he serious?

Bia did her best to focus on the work she had in front of her. Even though it was the start of a new weekly cycle for the paper's publication, she couldn't afford to get behind.

After the staff meeting where they talked about what they each had on the horizon and Bia had made various assignments of the things she knew were coming up that week, she went into her office to begin writing her editorial.

She had just pulled up the screen and poised her hands on the keyboard when her phone's intercom buzzed.

"Excuse me, Bia," said Candice. "Duane Beasley is here to see you."

She blinked at the computer screen, stunned and a little shaken. *Duane? What in the world?*

"Thank you, Candice," she said. "Please tell him to have a seat. I'll be out to see him in a few minutes."

Why? Why is Duane here? After they'd broken up, he'd taken a job in Boise, Idaho. He'd moved. Far away from her. Far away from the mess that their relationship had become. She hadn't heard from him in two years. What was he doing here?

She opened her purse, powdered her nose and reapplied her lipstick. Not that she wanted to look good for Duane; she simply wanted to look pulled together. She wanted to radiate confidence and let him know that she hadn't lost a single night's sleep since she'd discovered what a cheating sleazeball he was.

And to think she'd almost married him.

But she didn't.

He was sitting in a chair in the reception area. His dark head was bent, a sweep of hair falling across his forehead as he read the most recent edition of the

Dallas Journal of Business and Development when Bia approached.

He looked up, smiled and stood.

"Duane," Bia said. "My gosh, what are you doing here?"

"Hello, stranger," he said, blue eyes flashing in that way she used to find so irresistible. "Long time no see."

Dressed in khakis, a white business shirt and tie, he was still a good-looking guy; there was no doubt about it. Tall but not as thin as he used to be, when he'd played basketball in college. He was still fit, but it looked as if the less active business life was starting to catch up with him.

He walked toward her, and, for a moment, she thought he was going to hug her. So, she stuck her hand out, offering it instead. She hadn't exactly meant it as a handshake, more as a preemptive distance maker, allowing her to keep her personal space.

Because once she got past the eyes and the great smile that used to melt her heart, she couldn't forget that he had cheated on her.

Two nights before their wedding.

Bia's bridesmaids had called everyone on the guest list and told them not to come. The wedding was off.

It was the most heart-wrenching, humiliating time in her life.

Worse than the *XYZ* ambushes.

Yes. Even worse than that.

That's what she thought about as Duane stood there holding her hand in his. She politely pulled it away, took a step back and forced her best neutral smile. She didn't want him to think she was happy to see him, but she didn't want him to think she was unhappy. Neutrality was the best revenge. *I don't dislike you. That would take too much energy. I feel nothing for you.*

Except the need to find out why he was here and then get back to work.

"What can I do for you, Duane?"

"Wow, so formal," he said. "Bia, it's me. You don't have to be all businesslike. We're still friends, I hope?"

Okay, there was no way they were doing this here, out in the open, with Candice watching them, in this building where even the walls, no doubt, had ears.

"Can we go for a cup of coffee?" he asked. "For old time's sake."

"Not for old time's sake, but I can spare ten minutes if you want to go next door to the diner. Candice," Bia said, "I'm going out for a few moments."

Then she turned to Duane. "Wait here while I get my purse."

"Bia, I can buy you a cup of coffee," Duane said.

She waved him off as she started toward the door that separated the reception area from the newsroom. "I need to get my phone, anyway. I'll be right back."

When Bia turned around, she almost ran smack into Nicole.

"Oh!" Bia exclaimed, startled to see anyone standing there. But of course it would be Nicole.

Of course.

The woman stood blocking the doorway, looking back and forth between Duane and Bia.

Bia could virtually see the wheels in the woman's reporter's mind turning, doing the math to see if it added up to what the hunch that was probably gnawing at her gut right about now was suggesting to her. Bia knew what went on inside minds like Nicole's. She had once been not so dissimilar from her subordinate. In fact, that same sort of take-no-prisoners gut hunch was what had led her to the stories that had eventually won her the editorship of the paper.

But it just wasn't so comfortable when you were the victim of the hunch, Bia thought. "Excuse me, Nicole," Bia said. "Are you coming or going?"

"I was going," she said. "I have an interview with Brian Collins over at Collins Hardware. They're partnering with the bank to sponsor the Taste of Celebration this year. I was just heading out."

Bia stepped aside to let her pass. As she went through the door to the newsroom, she cast a quick glance over her shoulder and saw Nicole stop and introduce herself to Duane.

"You know what, Duane?" Bia said, interrupting the two midintroduction. "Why don't you just come back to my office? There's coffee in the break room. No sense in us going next door. I'm swamped today. I'm sure our business will be quick."

Duane shrugged and walked to stand next to Bia.

"Goodbye, Nicole," Bia said. "Have a great interview. I'll be eager to read your Taste of Celebration piece."

As they walked to Bia's office, Duane said, "So, you're in charge around here, huh?"

"I'm the editor, if that's what you mean."

He nodded as he looked around. Was that supposed to be approval? Irritation roiled in her gut.

"What's up, Duane? Did you just happen to be in the neighborhood? Just passing through? Celebration isn't exactly on your way from Idaho to much of anywhere."

Duane's hands were splayed on his knees. The way he was pitched forward in his seat made him look awkward. Or maybe even a little aggressive.

"I have business in Dallas," he said. "It's part of my territory."

"What are you doing these days?" She asked this in the spirit of making polite conversation, not out of personal interest.

"I'm a rep for Tilton Wholesale Tractor parts. I have the southeastern division."

Bia nodded stiffly. Her hands were folded on top of her desk, until she realized Duane was looking at her ring. She moved her hands to her lap.

"Is it true you and Aiden are engaged?"

Her thumb found the back of her ring and she traced it around to the stone in front. The real, fifteen-grand stone in the ring that Aiden had purchased and put on her finger.

"We are," she said, taking care to inject an enthusiastic upturn into her voice. "Don't tell me you came all this way to congratulate us."

Duane made a noise that was somewhere between a huff and a sigh. "What are you doing, Bia?"

Her email dinged, indicating the delivery of another message. It was the fifth notification she'd heard since they'd sat down in her office.

"Right now at this moment, not what I should be doing, considering today's long to-do list," she said.

She moved her mouse, activating her computer screen and glanced at her in-box. It wasn't that she wasn't glad to see him—

"I'm serious, Bia. Don't make a joke out of this."

She looked up from her in-box and skewered him with the most reproachful look she could conjure.

Why was she trying to be polite?

Actually, she wasn't happy to see Duane, to have him come barging back into her life, to have him sit in her office, taking up time she should be spending on the job she needed to do.

Who did he think he was? After what he'd done, what made him think he had the right?

"Duane, as a matter of fact, Aiden and I are engaged. But, frankly, it's none of your business. You don't get to come in here asking these questions, wearing that face that looks like you're about to tell me I'm making the biggest mistake of my life. I already came through the other side of the biggest mistake of my life. Been there, done that. I'd love to chat, but I have a lot to do."

She stood, hoping he would take the cue and do the same.

But he didn't. The big lunk sat there as if he had no intention of moving until he'd said what he came to say.

Great, this had the potential to get very uncomfortable. She regretted not going next door to the diner, where she could have walked away.

"Why would you want to marry a guy who caused your first wedding to be canceled?"

"What's done is done. We're not going to rehash the

past because it's not going to change anything. Aiden is a great guy. He's always looked out for me—"

"He wasn't looking out for you the night of my bachelor party." Duane's face had flushed. Bia had forgotten how that happened when he got mad.

"What *he* did the night of your bachelor party wasn't what caused us to call off the wedding. *You* were responsible for your own actions, Duane."

Duane stood and slammed his open palm down on Bia's desk. "Dammit, he set me up. He got me drunk and brought that prostitute in to climb all over me. I didn't know what I was doing."

Bia rolled her eyes. "You see, that's the thing about you, Duane—you've never been able to take responsibility for your actions. And, for the record, she wasn't a prostitute, she was a stripper. Aiden may have paid her to take her clothes off, but he didn't pay her to sleep with you. That was a deal you brokered all by yourself. So don't blame somebody else."

"He told you she was a stripper? Is that what he said? If so, your fiancé is lying through his teeth. I just thought you should know. Marrying him would be a bigger mistake than—"

"Than what, Duane? Losing you?"

Duane scrubbed his eyes with the heels of his hands, then raked his hands through his spiky dark hair.

"The guy will stop at nothing to get what he wants. The woman was a prostitute. He got me drunk and set me up. By doing that, he set you up, too. I just thought you ought to know before you made the biggest mistake of your life by marrying him."

Chapter Fourteen

Maya stood outside the Celebration Bed and Breakfast clutching the box of chocolates she'd finished making only an hour and a half ago.

She could've had one of her sales staff deliver it to Charles Jordan, but something wouldn't let her do it. This was a task she had to do herself.

When his order had come in that morning for a dozen salted caramels, with the request for them to be delivered at six o'clock that evening, she decided she would be the one to bring them to him. The order, which had come in five days after her hasty retreat from the pub, felt like a sign. Well, not just the order in itself, but the fact that it coincided with her finding a suitable substitute for the orange essence that she needed for the Borgia truffles.

Borgias had been Ian's favorites.

Maya felt like she was losing her mind, but after she had made the batch of Borgias, a strong gust of wind had blown open the kitchen door. It was a gust of wind she hadn't witnessed since she'd been away from St. Michel.

If she didn't know better, she might think that the winds of love had blown open her door to send a message—that she needed to open her heart and see what was standing right in front of her. Just as she had been telling her daughter to do with the man who was obviously her soul mate.

It was a lot scarier to take her own advice. Especially when she hadn't been able to feel anything remotely like what she'd been feeling since the last time she'd kissed Ian Brannigan goodbye nearly three decades ago.

Was it such a bad thing that Charles Jordan reminded her of Ian? The resemblance in personality was only a hasty assessment. She hadn't known the man very long. It wasn't such a bad thing that perhaps he possessed some of the qualities that Ian had possessed.

That's why she found herself attracted to him.

And there wasn't a thing wrong with that. It wasn't as if she was being disrespectful to Ian's memory. He wouldn't want her to spend the rest of her life mourning and longing for something that could never be.

Or at least that's what she told herself as she pulled open the door of the bed-and-breakfast and marched up to the front desk to let him know she was there.

He was down in the lobby in less than two minutes after Maria, the front desk receptionist, called his room.

She was relieved that he hadn't expected her to bring them up to the room. She'd already prepared an exit strategy: she would simply leave the box at the desk since he had prepaid for the candy.

Actually, it was another little test that she had tucked away in the back of her mind. If he came down to the lobby, it was a good sign and she would stay. If he asked her to bring them to the room, it was a bad sign and she would leave.

As Charles Jordan stood there looking at her through those too-familiar eyes, she knew in her heart of hearts that the winds of love had indeed blown into her kitchen and that she'd read the signs correctly.

"I'm so glad you came," Charles said.

Maya nodded and clutched the box in front of her, grateful she had something to do with her clumsy hands since she felt as awkward and shy as a schoolgirl.

Why was this so hard?

"Would you like to take a walk?" Charles asked. "We can leave the chocolates at the desk."

He must've sensed her uncertainty, because before she could even answer, he took the box from her and gave it to Maria to hold on to.

They walked side by side out into the early evening air.

"It's the perfect night for a walk," Charles said. "I've been dying to get outside all day. How is business today?"

Finally, Maya found her voice, thanks to how relaxed Charles was and how easy he was making their time together.

"It was good, busy," she said. "But I still found time to make your salted caramels and another surprise."

"A surprise? I love surprises." He slanted her a glance laced with a mischievous smile. "If I wasn't enjoying my time with you so much, I would be tempted to turn around and go back and see what the surprise is. That is, if you brought it."

"I did. They're in the box with your salted caramels. It's the funniest thing. The other day as I was placing an order with one of my suppliers, I came across an orange extract that looks like it could be a fair substitute for the one I used to use for the Borgias. They overnighted it to me. I tried it. And it is almost identical to the one that was discontinued. So not only did I order several cases of the extract, but I used the rest of the bottle to whip up a batch of Borgias."

Charles's brow shot up—another expression that made Maya weak in the knees.

"Are you telling me that I am one of the privileged few who gets to sample your first batch of Borgias after all these years?"

They had found their way to Central Park and were heading toward the gazebo.

"Yes, you are. And I expect an honest assessment. I need to know if they compare to the old tried-and-true. That is, if you can remember. It's been so long. How many years did you say?"

Her stomach did a loop-the-loop as she asked the question. Having been so tongue-tied earlier, she was having trouble keeping her filter in place.

"It's been twenty-nine years," Charles said. "And I still remember the taste of them as if it were yesterday. A man doesn't forget something that sweet and that special."

They were standing under the gazebo now, face-to-face, inches apart. Maya was vaguely aware of people walking past on the sidewalk a good ten yards away. They were there, but not really. All she could see was Charles, looking at her looking at him.

If she squinted her eyes, just enough to blur out the background, to soften the lines, he looked just like—

No.

She took a step back, turned and walked over to the gazebo's rail. She wasn't going to do this to herself. From this distance she could see Charles Jordan.

She needed to focus on *Charles Jordan.*

Not Ian Brannigan.

Charles Jordan.

Charles must have sensed the shift in her mood, because he walked over to the same rail that Maya was leaning against, but he left a good bit of space between the two of them.

"Isn't Facebook a wonderful thing?" he asked. "I was thrilled when I found you online."

If she analyzed his words, he might have sounded a little like a stalker. But he didn't scare her.

"Is that so? How long have you been following me? And should I be worried about that?"

He laughed. "Oh, dear God, I hope you're not worried about it. I promise, I'm harmless. That's why I've stayed away for so long."

Maya's heart started drumming a rapid staccato.

She could hear it in her ears. That's when she realized she'd been holding her breath. She exhaled.

"What do you mean?" she asked, unsure if she wanted to hear the answer.

Charles leaned back on the rail and crossed one foot over the other.

"Twenty-nine years ago, Ian Brannigan was in the wrong place at the wrong time."

All the blood drained from Maya's head, and her peripheral vision went a little white and hazy. She gripped the gazebo's wooden railing as she waited for him to continue. She wanted to ask, *How did you know Ian?* But she couldn't dislodge the words from her throat.

"He witnessed a crime that left him injured and in need of protection. Not only for his own safety, but for the safety of those he loved."

"No, that's not right," Maya said. The words sounded like they were coming from outside her body. "Ian was killed in an accident. His mother told me…."

Charles was looking at her with pleading eyes.

No…it couldn't be. Maya wouldn't let herself believe what she was thinking. If she dredged up the hope that she'd buried so long ago and let herself believe even for a second of a second…and then it turned out that he was…

"Death from the accident was exactly what UK Protected Persons Services wanted everyone to believe. And there was an accident. A terribly disfiguring accident. As far as the world was concerned, Ian Brannigan was dead. But—"

"Ian?"

He nodded. "God, how I've missed you, love."

In an instant she was in his arms. His lips were on hers; his hands were in her hair.

And she knew.

Even after all those years, after all that time apart, looking so different, he still tasted the same and she still fit perfectly in his arms. He was the piece of the puzzle, the piece of her heart that had been missing for nearly thirty years.

Breathlessly, she pulled away, bracing herself to wake from a dream—a dream she'd had so many nights she'd lost track. The dream would be so real; she could feel him, taste him. He was always so alive and then morning's light—the thief that it was—would steal him away. She'd wake up alone with the phantom ache in the place where her heart used to be.

Tonight, with a symphony of cicadas playing in the background and the perfume of night-blooming jasmine in the air, she opened her eyes and Ian was still there. She clung to him as tears streamed down her face.

"Please tell me this is real. Even after all these years, you're not gone. You're really here."

He answered her with a kiss that she felt all the way down to her toes. When he finally released her, she drank him in with her eyes. Her finger traced the scar at his collar.

She had so many questions.

"But why? What happened to you, Ian?"

He told her the story of how when he met her he had been doing undercover work for Interpol. He had been caught in the cross fire of an organized crime operation that he had been trying to take down for several months. In the process, his car had gone off a rocky cliff between Monaco and Nice, France. He had been hurt badly. In fact, he had been close to death. That's when his superiors had made the decision to declare him dead and give him a new identity for his protection and that of those he loved.

"It was too dangerous," he said. "I couldn't subject you and my family to the harm that those sociopaths would've inflicted upon you, your family, my family in the blink of an eye. So they declared me dead, rebuilt my face and gave me a new identity in a new country. The work I had done coupled with the ongoing investigation had helped send away the heads of the criminal organization. Last month, the last dangerous person associated with that organization was executed. It's finally safe enough for me to contact you without putting you in danger."

"Does it mean that we can be together?"

"If you're willing to give Charles Jordan a chance, yes. Ian Brannigan is legally dead."

"No, he's not," said Maya. "He's very much alive in my heart. I just hope that Charles Jordan is willing to hear what I have to say. Because he's missed out on a lot over the twenty-nine years he's been gone."

"We need to talk," Bia said when Aiden got home from work that evening.

The shoot had gone later than he'd planned. They were already over budget for the month, and they still had a week left to go. He was hungry and tired and a little edgy. All he wanted was an ice-cold beer and a kiss from this woman who was becoming the center of his universe.

We need to talk was not what he wanted to hear when he walked in the door.

She was sitting on the far side of the sofa in the shadows of the living room, which was lit by only one small table lamp. She had her feet curled underneath her, and she looked incredibly small sitting there all alone in the dim room.

Aiden immediately knew that something was wrong.

"Is everything all right? Is the baby okay?"

All the possibilities of all the things that could go wrong collided in his head with the result of a fifty-car pileup.

"The baby's fine. But I had a visitor today. Sit down and I'll tell you about it. There's a lot that we need to talk about."

Hugh's family? They were the first ones to pop into his head. Had that attorney—what was his name? Had he told the family and had they come to say they wanted to be part of the child's life?

"Duane came to see me today."

"Duane Beasley?"

That was almost as bad as Hugh's family.

"What did he want?"

"To tell me that you set him up the night of the bachelor party."

Ah, man. Not this again.

He raked his hand through his hair, reminding himself to watch his tone. He shouldn't take out his irritation on Bia. He was hungry, he was irritable and he was tired of this same subject.

"We've been round and round about this, Bia. Duane is a big boy. He's responsible for his own actions. What the heck was he doing here? Thought he lived in Ohio or somewhere like that?"

"He lives in Idaho. But he travels with his job. That's why he was here. He was in Dallas on business. Aiden, did you hire a prostitute to seduce Duane?"

She'd never phrased the question quite that way before. The question had always been whether he set Duane up. Not if he had specifically hired someone with the express purpose of seducing him.

Ah, man. He wasn't going to lie to her.

"Well, I have never hired a prostitute. I hired a dancer for Duane's bachelor party. There's a fine line in that profession. I'm not saying that all dancers or even most dancers are prostitutes. But sometimes they cross the line."

"Aiden, cut to the chase. Did you ask the woman to seduce my fiancé?"

Before he'd always managed to nip this conversation in the bud with the fact that Duane had free will. Tonight Bia was asking another question. Had he asked the woman to seduce Duane?

He looked up at the ceiling. His pulse was pounding in his temples. His blood was rushing in his ears. He looked down at his shoes, weighing his words. Finally he looked back at Bia. Into those eyes that were dark with pain and questions.

Damn that bastard.

"Even if he had a naked woman crawling on him, he should've said no," said Aiden.

"Aiden, just answer my question. Yes or no? Did you tell her to seduce him?"

He could tell that she read it in his eyes even before he could say the word. She scooted to the edge of the couch. Her palms were braced on the cushions on either side of her.

"Aiden, you were married to Tracey at the time. Why did you do it? Why did you set up Duane? Got him drunk, hired a woman to put it in his face? Why would you do that to me?"

"Bia, why would you want a man who would be unfaithful to you?"

"That's beside the point right now. I trusted you, Aiden. I trusted you to take my fiancé out, not to sabotage my marriage. And what about your marriage, Aiden? Why would you do this?"

"Bia, Tracey and I were already separated at this point—"

"So you wanted to break up Duane and me, too? Why? Because misery loves company."

"No, that's not what it was. It wasn't the first time that Duane had cheated on you. I just didn't want to see you get stuck with someone who didn't deserve you. Because you have always deserved so much more."

He wanted to say, "Because I've always loved you," but the words were stuck in his throat.

God, man-up.

"Who made you the morals police?"

"I've loved you my entire life. I realized it too late.

Or at least I thought it was too late, until now. We don't have to keep being the star-crossed lovers, Bia. We can do this."

She took off the diamond ring, set it on the coffee table and gave it a shove. It sailed toward him, went off the end of the table and landed at his feet.

Then she sat back in the corner of the couch, drew her knees up under her chin and wrapped her arms around them. "Just go, Aiden. It's too late for us."

The next morning Bia awoke to the sound of a ringing phone. The first thought that went through her head was, *Aiden?*

Oh, please let it be Aiden. But it wasn't. It was Maya.

"Hello?"

"Good morning, sunshine," Maya virtually sang into the phone.

Bia glanced at the clock. It was seven o'clock. She'd overslept. She'd have to hurry or she'd be late for work. Even so, phone pressed to her ear, she rolled over onto her back and threw her arm over her eyes.

"Good morning," she said, not even trying to infuse the slightest enthusiasm into her voice.

"Did I wake you up?" Maya asked. "I thought you would be up already. Don't you have to work today?"

"Yeah, I do. I had a rough night last night."

"I'm sorry. Were you feeling sick again?"

"No, Aiden and I broke up. I mean, if you can even call it that. If we were even together. I gave him back the ring."

"What happened?" Maya asked, alarm apparent in her voice.

"It's a long story. Maybe we can meet for lunch and I'll tell you. I could use some advice. Speaking of, you never gave me the Charles Jordan report."

There was a long pause.

"Are you there?" Bia asked.

"I am," Maya answered. "Funny you should mention that. Because I do have news."

"Good news?" Bia asked.

"Very good."

"What? Were you going to wait for me to drag it out of you?"

"I wasn't sure if you were up for it right now given the situation with Aiden."

Bia rolled onto her stomach. "Please, I'm dying for some good news. In fact, would you like to meet for breakfast? I'm not feeling exceptionally motivated this morning. Maybe your happiness will jump-start my day. Wow. Maybe I can start living vicariously through my mother."

Bia had to stop by the office before she met Maya. She just had to run in to take care of one call. She'd left the number on her desk.

Good grief, she was scattered. She needed to get herself together and get her head back in the game. Easier said than done, when her heart was heavy with regret.

She'd slept fitfully, waking up every few hours and wondering if she'd done the right thing giving the ring back to Aiden. And the conclusion she came to was of course she had. It wasn't a real engagement, despite the ring and the proposal and the chemistry between them. The fact remained that the only reason he had proposed was to save her from the *XYZ* scumbag.

She didn't need saving.

Maybe she needed to prove that to herself as much as anyone.

Problem was, she had started to believe their PR. If it was going to end sometime, it might as well be now. She hadn't seen or heard from the *XYZ* reporter since Maya had chased him out of her shop. He had probably decided that there was no news here. At least not the kind of news he got paid for raking up. No doubt he was somewhere else turning over rocks to see what would jump out. *Good riddance.*

On her way to work, she thought of something funny and immediately reached for her phone to call Aiden. Then she didn't.

This was exactly the thing that she didn't want to happen. Now everything was messed up. Now she felt weird about calling him for the least little thing like she used to. Because now the least little thing seemed like a big inconvenience.

Not only that, but she needed some space to get him out of her system. That's what you got when you played with fire. You got burned.

But no one was going to save her from this fire but herself.

She parked and made her way into her office, dropping her purse on the credenza behind her desk. As she was moving papers around, looking for the scrap of paper with the number she needed, she noticed Nicole standing in the doorway.

"Did you need something?" Bia asked.

"Where's your ring?" Nicole asked.

Bia glanced at her finger as if she expected to see it there. Of course she didn't, but she wasn't in the mood to deal with Nicole. "It's not there, is it? Don't you have something you need to do? Should I find something for you to write about?"

By now she sounded like the Wicked Witch of the West. But her snark had done the trick. Nicole frowned at her and turned around and walked away.

Within fifteen minutes, Bia was walking into the diner next door to her office. The hostess greeted her with a warm, cheery smile and asked how many would be in her party. Bia spied Maya's red curls across the restaurant.

"Thanks, but I see my party right over there," she said.

She was halfway to the booth when she noticed that Maya was sitting with a man. Bia stopped and did a double take.

That must be Charles Jordan.

Good, Bia thought, she could use a little show-and-tell distraction to boost her mood. Plus, meeting the guy in person she'd be able to get a better read on him to make sure he had good intentions. The place she was in, he better be honorable or she'd personally run him out of town on a rail.

The phrase struck her as funny. She made a mental note to look up the origin of that term when she got back to the office. In the meantime, she put on her best smile and her most generous attitude. If this man made her mother happy, she would be his biggest supporter. She whispered a silent prayer that at least one of them could be lucky in love.

When Maya looked up and saw Bia approaching, she waved. Her hazel eyes were sparkling. She seemed to be glowing with happiness. *Well, somebody must've gotten lucky,* Bia thought. It wasn't quite apparent whether it was in love or lust. Either way Maya was smitten, and Bia's mood was instantly buoyed.

The man stood as she approached. He was tall with dark hair and blue eyes. He had a great smile. Her first impression was that he had a kind face. Bia knew it was early to tell, but something about him made her confident that he was just as smitten with Maya as she was with him.

Maya threw her arms around Bia.

"Um…*Charles,*" Maya looked up at the man and made a face that seemed to indicate that they were sharing some sort of inside joke. "Charles, this is Bia."

Maya closed her eyes for a moment and took Bia's hand.

Tears were in Maya's eyes, but she was smiling so they looked like happy tears. Bia hoped. This Charles had better not have done anything to make her mother cry—

Maya gave Bia's hand a quick squeeze. She took a deep breath, then said, "You don't know how long I have dreamed of saying this. Bia, I would like to introduce you to your father."

Her father?
Her father.

In the span of less than three weeks, she'd not only gained a mother, but a father, too.

It was a little hard to wrap her mind around. But Bia had meant it when she'd said she would be genuinely happy for her mother if things worked out.

And they had worked out in a way that Bia had never imagined.

Charles was the only man Maya had ever loved. Her love for him had withstood nearly thirty years of separation, of giving up a child, of no other man ever measuring up.

Her mind drifted back to Aiden and when he'd told her that she was the only woman he had ever loved. She wanted to believe that but…

How could he love her? She was pregnant with another man's child.

This whole thing had started as a farce. It had blossomed out of the game of chase, of Bia being a challenge. If she put some distance between them now, there might be a chance to save their friendship.

She felt almost panicky thinking about life without Aiden.

Yes, she would fix this, somehow. Just not now. They needed time.

She finished the editorial that had taken her way too long to write. It wasn't stellar, but at least it was done. The words were on paper. She could come back to it and visit it again tomorrow. For now she had to get out of this place.

It was already seven o'clock. It was starting to get

dusky outside. She still needed to stop by the grocery store. She might as well call it a day.

The problem was, she didn't want to go home. The house was cold and empty without Aiden. She wished that they could turn back the clock to the time when things were good.

She wanted to tell him about her father. Heck, she wanted him to meet her father. Wanted her father to meet him. But why? What were they to each other now?

This is my friend, Aiden.

This is my almost lover and former fiancé, Aiden.

This is my pretend fiancé and former friend, Aiden.

None of it felt right. None of it made sense anymore.

She missed him. But she'd messed that up pretty good, hadn't she?

Since she was the last person out of the building, she locked the door. She set her laptop bag and her purse down while she struggled to maneuver the tricky lock. When she finally got the dead bolt to turn, she picked up her things and turned around to leave. She nearly jumped out of her skin at the sight of the all-too-familiar and very much unwelcome face.

"Yo, Bia. Joey Camps from *XYZ Celebrity News.* How ya doin' today, darlin'?"

He trained the video camera on her.

How the heck did this guy do that? Sneak up behind her like that?

"Hey, Bia, where's your ring?"

God! How did this guy know these things? Who was telling him—

Nicole.

The realization came over her in ice-cold waves.

Oh, my God. It has to be Nicole.

She'd been there when Bia had first interviewed Hugh. Nicole had commented on Bia's getting sick in the bathroom. She'd asked her if she'd had a rough night out. Nicole had known Bia was out of the office for a doctor's appointment because Bia had casually mentioned it at the staff meeting. She hadn't realized she'd need to be vague about her whereabouts. It wouldn't have been hard for Nicole to figure out which doctor Bia had gone to. The woman seemed to turn up almost as much as Joey Camps. But Bia would never have been able to put it together if not for Nicole questioning her today about the ring.

Of course. It had to be Nicole.

"So, Joey, did Nicole call you again?"

For a brief moment, Bia saw a flash of recognition in Joey's eyes. Not the look of confusion that would have been there had Nicole not been his informant.

Good old Joey Camps didn't have a very good poker face.

"So, no ring, huh?" Joey asked. "Does this mean the wedding's off?"

How ironic—just yesterday she'd resented Aiden for always trying to come to her rescue. She'd been so adamant about saving herself. About trust and truth and everything she ever thought was good and real and right.

And then today she'd met her father.

A man that Maya had thought dead for nearly thirty years.

So what did it all mean?

What was truth? The things you grew up with? The father who had never bothered to tell her she was adopted? Did that make him any less of a father? Because Charles had been in her life less than twenty-four hours, did that discount him?

Because Aiden had always been her friend, did that mean he couldn't be her lover—her husband?

Did it make any difference how Aiden had exposed Duane for the cheater that he was? Once a cheater, always a cheater, right?

Everything was upside down.

"Since the engagement's off, does it mean that Hugh's your baby daddy, Bia?" Joey whined.

She suddenly realized that she could be tossed and turned by the changes that were taking place or she could grab the wheel of her life and steer it in the direction that she wanted it to go.

"Hey, Joey, I'll make a deal with you. Let me put my purse in the car and I'll give you an interview you will never forget. Just let me set these things down. They're heavy."

"Cool. I'm down with that."

Bia put her things in the car and her keys in her pocket, and rolled up her sleeves. She picked up the garden hose that was lying in its usual heap on the asphalt, turned it on at the spigot—

"Hey, what are you doing?" Joey cried as she drenched him and his camera with water.

Chapter Fifteen

Every time someone new entered the shop, Bia's heart gave a little lurch. Tonight was the party that Maya had originally planned as a post–grand opening celebration—once she got the kinks worked out of the day-to-day operations.

Now that she was ready to show off her shop, the party had morphed into a triple celebration: the shop's opening; the reunion of Bia, Maya and Charles; and an engagement party for Maya and Charles. After all this time the two would finally be married.

Bia owed it to her mom—to her parents....She hadn't yet gotten used to calling them that. She really truly was happy for them, even if she was still mourning the loss of her relationship with Aiden. She was hoping he would come tonight. He'd been invited.

As a matter of fact, Maya had invited him herself. But so far he was a no-show.

Bia's heart ached, but she'd be damned if she would let the smile slip from her face and ruin what should otherwise be a very happy occasion.

The key was to keep busy. She was helping A.J., Pepper, Caroline and Sydney keep the hors d'oeuvres stocked and circulating. She helped fill champagne glasses and made sure that the dessert table was stocked with plenty of Maya's chocolates. If being an editor didn't work out, she figured she could always get a job as a waitress. She cajoled herself with the thought that she sort of had a knack for it.

She was back in the kitchen restocking a tray when Drew walked in. "So I hear your friend was back the other day. The *XYZ* reporter? Is that what you call him? A reporter?"

"Why don't you ask Nicole? I'm almost positive she's the one who has been feeding him information."

Drew's nostrils flared. "Are you kidding? Do you know this for a fact?"

Bia leaned on the counter, looking him squarely in the eyes. "I can't say that I have any hard factual evidence. It's mostly circumstantial. But she really does fit the part. I started detailing all of the events and who might've known. She's the common denominator in all of them. So let's just call it a very strong hunch. The same kind of hunch that helped me help you bring down Texas Star."

Drew stroked his chin contemplatively. "Should you fire her? It is considered conflict of interest if she's giving news to other sources. She signed a no-compete agreement when she came on board."

Bia sighed. "I don't know, Drew. I'll have to think about it. Although, at the next staff meeting, I will review the no-compete agreements and make sure that everyone understands exactly what it means."

"Good idea."

Bia stared down at her naked left hand, at the place where the ring used to adorn her finger. Now it was as empty as she felt.

She looked up a little sheepishly. "Have you talked to Aiden?"

"As a matter of fact, I have. He's taking it pretty hard. He loves you, Bia. If you ever want to talk about what happened…I'm not really good with that kind of advice, but I can listen."

Bia gave him a rueful smile. "And I'm not really good at talking about things like that. So, I don't know if we'd make a very good counselor–patient team. But thanks, anyway. I appreciate the thought."

"At the risk of sounding like I'm giving advice," said Drew. "Talk to him. Tell him how you feel. I think you might be surprised at how much you two think alike."

Actually, no, she wouldn't be surprised. She and Aiden had always been simpatico. What had happened to them?

They'd crossed that line. Now it felt like there was no turning back.

Maya appeared in the doorway. "There you are!" she sang in her lyrical accented English. "Come, come! We need you out here *tout de suite.*"

"This sounds urgent," said Drew. "Leave the tray. Caroline will help me fill it when the quiches are done. You go ahead and see what Maya needs. This is your night—well, yours and your family's. Why are you working?"

Because if I don't keep busy I'll make myself crazy.

Bia smoothed her hair, checked the front of her black cocktail dress for crumbs and went to see why Maya needed her so urgently.

When Bia stepped out onto the shop floor, the crowd parted, revealing Aiden at the center.

He smiled when he saw her. And her entire body gave in to the feeling of relief seeing him there. Her first impulse was to walk up and put her arms around him and kiss him senseless, but then she remembered they hadn't even talked since the night she'd given him the ring back.

"There you are," he said. "I have something to ask you."

Bia glanced around, fully aware that everyone was watching them. "Here?"

"Absolutely. This is something all of our friends and family need to see." He walked up to her, took her hand in his and dropped down on one knee.

"Bia Anderson, will you do me the great honor of being my wife?"

The room was so quiet, Bia was sure everyone could hear her labored breathing and the beating of her heart.

Oh, my gosh, what is he doing?

She glanced from Aiden to Maya, who was nodding vigorously, to Charles. "I've already asked your parents for your hand. They said yes."

He was holding the ring between his left thumb and index finger. The brilliant diamond sparkled as if it were connected to an energy source.

She leaned in and said, "Can we talk in private?"

Ever the eternal optimist, Aiden pacified himself with the fact that she didn't say no. Of course, she could be talking to him in private so as not to hurt his feelings, but they were too good together. This time he was not going to let her go. He knew she loved him as much as he loved her. He just did not know what the problem was. He had a feeling he was about to find out.

He followed Bia into the kitchen and up a set of stairs that he didn't know existed in the shop. They led up to what seemed to be Maya's sleeping quarters.

He glanced around the cozy space. A Murphy bed adorned one wall, and a small love seat and chair grouped around a coffee table in the center of the room.

Bia chose the love seat. Aiden sat down next to her.

"Aiden, what are you doing?"

"Last I checked, I had proposed to you. I guess the most accurate answer would be that I am waiting for you to answer me."

"But why?" she asked.

"Bia, I told you once, but I'll tell you again. Hell, I will tell you every day for the rest of our lives. I have never loved a woman the way that I love you. So it's only natural that I would want to spend the rest of my life with you."

"Doesn't it bother you that I'm pregnant with another man's baby?"

"I want a family, Bia. The baby's birth father is dead. I don't know what I would've done if it hadn't been for your father stepping in and serving as a role model for me."

She straightened. "So, wait, are you marrying me out of duty—paying back some perceived debt—or because you love me and want to spend the rest of your life with me?"

"Did you not hear me? I've never loved anyone but you. It's always been you. Well, except for the time I fell in love with my kindergarten teacher. But she wouldn't marry me because she already had a husband."

She smiled and shook her head, love apparent in her eyes. "Yeah, you've always been a player."

"So come play with me, Princess." He dropped down on one knee. "Come play with me for the rest of our lives. Will you?"

"Nothing would make me happier. I love you, Aiden."

They made their way back downstairs. Everyone hushed as they walked into the room.

"She said yes!" Aiden said.

He pulled his bride-to-be into his arms and sealed the deal.

* * * * *

COMING NEXT MONTH FROM

HARLEQUIN®

SPECIAL EDITION

Available April 15, 2014

#2329 THE PRINCE'S CINCERELLA BRIDE
The Bravo Royales • by Christine Rimmer
Lani Vasquez cherishes her role as nanny to the Montedoran royal children—particularly since it offers proximity to her good friend, the handsome Prince Maximilian. Max has grieved his lost wife for years, but this Prince Charming is ready for the next chapter of his love story—and his Cinderella is right under his nose.

#2330 FALLING FOR FORTUNE
The Fortunes of Texas: Welcome to Horseback Hollow
by Nancy Robards Thompson
Christopher Fortune has gladly embraced the wealth and power of his newfound family name. But not everyone's as impressed by the Fortune legacy. His new coworker, Kinsley Aaron, worked for everything she ever got, and Chris's newly entitled attitude rubs her the wrong way. Now Chris will have to earn Kinsley's love—and his Fortune fairy-tale ending....

#2331 THE HUSBAND LIST
Rx for Love • by Cindy Kirk
Great job? Check. Hunky hubby? Not so much. Dr. Mitzi Sanchez has her life just where she wants it—except for the husband she's always dreamed of. She creates a checklist for her perfect man—but she insists pilot Keenan McGregor isn't it. With a bit of luck, Keenan might blow Mitzi's expectations sky-high....

#2332 HEALED WITH A KISS
Bride Mountain • by Gina Wilkins
Both burned by love, wedding planner Alexis Mosley and innkeeper Logan Carmichael aren't looking for anything serious when they plunge into a passionate affair. Little by little, though, what starts as a no-strings-attached fling evolves into something much deeper. Can they heal their emotional wounds to start afresh, or will the ghosts of relationships past haunt them forever?

#2333 GROOMED FOR LOVE
Sweet Springs, Texas • by Helen R. Myers
Due to her declining sight, Rylie Quinn abandoned her dreams of becoming a veterinarian and moved to Sweet Springs, Texas, as an animal groomer. She just wants to get on with her life—something that irritating attorney Noah Prescott won't allow her to do. He's determined to dig up Rylie's past, and, as he and Rylie butt heads, true love might just rear its own.

#2334 THE BACHELOR DOCTOR'S BRIDE
The Doctors MacDowell • by Caro Carson
Bright, free-spirited and bubbly, Diana Connor gets under detached cardiologist Quinn MacDowell's skin...and not in a way he'd care to admit. When the two are forced to work together at a field clinic, Quinn begins to see just how caring Diana is and how well she interacts with patients. This heart doctor might just need a bit of Diana's medicine for himself....

_____

**YOU CAN FIND MORE INFORMATION ON UPCOMING HARLEQUIN® TITLES,
FREE EXCERPTS AND MORE AT WWW.HARLEQUIN.COM.**

HSECNM0414

REQUEST YOUR FREE BOOKS!

2 FREE NOVELS PLUS 2 FREE GIFTS!

⊕ HARLEQUIN®

SPECIAL EDITION

Life, Love & Family

YES! Please send me 2 FREE Harlequin® Special Edition novels and my 2 FREE gifts (gifts are worth about $10). After receiving them, if I don't wish to receive any more books, I can return the shipping statement marked "cancel." If I don't cancel, I will receive 6 brand-new novels every month and be billed just $4.74 per book in the U.S. or $5.24 per book in Canada. That's a savings of at least 14% off the cover price! It's quite a bargain! Shipping and handling is just 50¢ per book in the U.S. and 75¢ per book in Canada.* I understand that accepting the 2 free books and gifts places me under no obligation to buy anything. I can always return a shipment and cancel at any time. Even if I never buy another book, the two free books and gifts are mine to keep forever.

235/335 HDN F45Y

Name _____ (PLEASE PRINT) _____

Address _____ Apt. # _____

City _____ State/Prov. _____ Zip/Postal Code _____

Signature (if under 18, a parent or guardian must sign)

Mail to the Harlequin® Reader Service:
IN U.S.A.: P.O. Box 1867, Buffalo, NY 14240-1867
IN CANADA: P.O. Box 609, Fort Erie, Ontario L2A 5X3

Want to try two free books from another line?
Call 1-800-873-8635 or visit www.ReaderService.com.

* Terms and prices subject to change without notice. Prices do not include applicable taxes. Sales tax applicable in N.Y. Canadian residents will be charged applicable taxes. Offer not valid in Quebec. This offer is limited to one order per household. Not valid for current subscribers to Harlequin Special Edition books. All orders subject to credit approval. Credit or debit balances in a customer's account(s) may be offset by any other outstanding balance owed by or to the customer. Please allow 4 to 6 weeks for delivery. Offer available while quantities last.

Your Privacy—The Harlequin® Reader Service is committed to protecting your privacy. Our Privacy Policy is available online at www.ReaderService.com or upon request from the Harlequin Reader Service.

We make a portion of our mailing list available to reputable third parties that offer products we believe may interest you. If you prefer that we not exchange your name with third parties, or if you wish to clarify or modify your communication preferences, please visit us at www.ReaderService.com/consumerschoice or write to us at Harlequin Reader Service Preference Service, P.O. Box 9062, Buffalo, NY 14269. Include your complete name and address.

HSEI3R

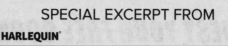
Lani Vasquez is a nanny to the royal children of Montedoro...and nothing more, or so she thinks. But widower Prince Maximilian Bravo-Calabretti hasn't forgotten their single passionate encounter. Can the handsome prince and the alluring au pair turn one night into forever? Or will their love turn Lani into a pumpkin at the stroke of midnight?

***

He was fresh out of new tactics and had no clue how to get her to let down her guard. Plus he had a very strong feeling that he'd pushed her as far as she would go for now. This was looking to be an extended campaign. He didn't like that, but if it was the only way to finally reach her, so be it. "I'll be seeing you in the library—where you will no longer scuttle away every time I get near you."

A hint of the old humor flashed in her eyes. "I never scuttle."

"Scamper? Dart? Dash?"

"Stop it." Her mouth twitched. A good sign, he told himself.

"Promise me you won't run off the next time we meet."

The spark of humor winked out. "I just don't like this."

"You've already said that. I'm going to show you there's nothing to be afraid of. Do we have an understanding?"

"Oh, Max..."

"Say yes."

And finally, she gave in and said the words he needed to hear. "Yes. I'll, um, look forward to seeing you."

He didn't believe her. How could he believe her when she sounded so grim, when that mouth he wanted beneath his own was twisted with resignation? He didn't believe her, and he almost wished he could give her what she said she wanted, let her go, say goodbye. He almost wished he could *not* care.

But he'd had so many years of not caring. Years and years when he'd told himself that not caring was for the best.

And then the small, dark-haired woman in front of him changed everything.

***

Enjoy this sneak peek from Christine Rimmer's
THE PRINCE'S CINDERELLA BRIDE,
*the latest installment in her Harlequin® Special Edition
miniseries* **THE BRAVO ROYALES,** *on sale May 2014!*

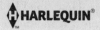

SPECIAL EDITION

Life, Love and Family

Coming in May 2014

HEALED WITH A KISS
by reader-favorite author
Gina Wilkins

Both burned by love, wedding planner Alexis Mosley and innkeeper Logan Carmichael aren't looking for anything serious when they plunge into a passionate affair. Little by little, though, what starts as a no-strings-attached fling evolves into something much deeper. Can they heal their emotional wounds to start afresh, or will the ghosts of relationships past haunt them forever?

Don't miss the third edition of the
Bride Mountain trilogy!

Available now from the
Bride Mountain trilogy by Gina Wilkins:

MATCHED BY MOONLIGHT
A PROPOSAL AT THE WEDDING

www.Harlequin.com

HSE65814